THE YOUNG WRITERS LITERARY JOURNAL

Edited by Nathaniel Lee Caldwell
Edited by Brad Stanley

Cover Art by Adam Singletary

YOUNG WRITERS SOCIETY PUBLISHERS
Bethesda

This is a work of fiction. Names, characters, places, and incidents are products of the authors' imagination or are used fictitiously and are not to be construed as real. Any resemblance to actual events, locales, organizations, or persons, living or dead, is entirely coincidental.

Young Writers Society Publishers

Bethesda, MD

www.YoungWritersSociety.com

ISBN: 978-0-6151-9577-3

First Edition: March 2008

Printed in the United States of America

TABLE OF CONTENTS

COPYRIGHT AND ACKNOWLEDGEMENTS

PREFACE

Brad Stanley

Today, and perhaps now more than ever before, we take the power of immediacy for granted. With just a few clicks of the mouse, we can be anywhere, looking at anything or buying items only travelers could purchase not twenty years ago. We experience life on-demand like an HBO special, and often at the terrible price of reflexivity, memory and longing.

Children have, in this sense, always been what anchor us to the ground. Their lack of boundaries and their desire to experience everything reminds us— sometimes frustratingly—that immediacy is not the be-all-end-all of existence. Writing, too, delivers us back to that womb of pre-natal experience: unlike the split-second of an image, the story still waits to be unfolded, and its discovery rests squarely on our shoulders and our ability to stumble through the universe created by the author.

What one finds in the pages that follow is the combination of these two elements: immensely gifted young people and their writing. Some poems, like "Treacle," are light-hearted and remind us to savor the good things in life, while others, like the elegiac "Sylvia," display a deep appreciation of those voices that have spoken before ours. Likewise, I was only too delighted to have been given the opportunity to read and review the stories. They, like the poetry, range from the rollicking romp of magical penguins to an eye-opened awareness of international struggles to the tiny wars we have at home and with ourselves. In this lies their beauty, and thus their power to change: they are voices that, while not always world-weary, brim with a keenness for human interaction and observation that will, doubtless, lead them to success. Indeed, the true measure of success is not how many times we get it right, but how many times we fall and pick ourselves back up, and as any artist or author can readily assure you, this happens only all too often in this business.

With that said, I hope you will enjoy what follows at least as much as I have. While each work chronicles particular events in our lives, I believe the anthology itself is a kind of documentation and testament to the resilience of the human condition. Our ability even when we are young to discern from the world kernels of truth and awe-inspiring tragedy and beauty marks this collection with a fervor I have not seen in any other publication for the young writer.

INTRODUCTION
Nathaniel Lee Caldwell

There is a quote that I am quite fond of by Anne Lamott, an American novelist. "We are a species that needs and wants to understand who we are. Sheep lice do not seem to share this longing, which is one reason why they write so little." Over the years, it has become the semi-official quote of the Young Writers Society.

For those who are not familiar with the Young Writers Society (YWS), it is a web-based message board dedicated to promoting creative writing as a pastime. Its audience consists primarily of those in high-school and college who not only enjoy creative writing, but also take pleasure from being an instructor to those who are just beginning to enter the craft. Thus, ages on the site range from as young as 13 to as old as 25, though there are certainly many members who fall outside that range.

Having begun in mid-November 2004, the site has succeeded because of a committed membership and dedicated volunteers. Without these people, this anthology would not have been possible, and while it certainly is not possible to thank everyone, I shall at least try to thank as many as possible.

First, I shall like to thank David Davenport, the administrator of the Young Writers Club, to which YWS is the proud successor. The Young Writers Club (TYWC) began in 1996, and David, along with his daughter, Derya, ran the site for many years as a place for young writers from across the world to convene. Not only was the site very international in scope (David operated TYWC from Turkey), but the site demonstrated early on the power of the internet to bring people of disparate cultures and diverse personalities together.

Second would of course be my parents, French and Patricia. Without their support, both verbal and financial, this anthology surely would have never happened. I have always, and will always, consider myself fortunate to have such loving and supportive individuals as my parents. It would be an honor just to know them, much less to be one of their offspring.

Third, there is of course Brad Stanley, who is my co-editor in this work and without whom I may have given up the enterprise altogether in late 2007. While I was studying for my finals as a first year law student at the Columbus School of Law in Washington, DC, he reviewed each submission, notified authors of the status of their submission, and even provided constructive criticism for those who saw their work denied. He has acted as managing editor of this work, leaving me free to concentrate on putting this together in book form. Without him, the task would be too daunting.

Finally, there are so many more individuals who I have to thank. There is Jack Dent and Rebekah Hart, who work hard at managing the site as co-administrators. Both of them have also lent their editing skills to this anthology, ensuring that grammatical missteps are kept to a minimum. There is also Karina, Suzanne, and Via, all of whom help significantly with YWS' various side activities such as Squills, our bi-monthly e-zine, and our blog. The latter three also all have some of their work appearing in this anthology.

There is also the entire moderating group at YWS, affectionately called Big Brother, who have done an excellent job at handling various conflicts and emergencies over the years. Then there are literally dozens of other members, possibly hundreds, who have helped at various points over the years. These people, though sometimes quite young, take on positions of responsibility within the community as Junior Moderators, Instructors, and Greeters. While I cannot thank everyone by name, make no mistake that no contribution has been so small as to be insignificant and that my thanks to you exceeds my limited ability to convey.

So as you the reader begin to turn the pages of this anthology, keep in mind that this is unlike any anthology you have read before. These works are not the self-obsessed, cynical wanderings of the forty year old disgruntled poet, but nor are they the polished masterpieces of the New Yorker or Atlantic Monthly.

Rather, the works you will find within is what I always have considered to be art in its purest form; as the raw, unpolished works of those who are just discovering the joy of engaging their mind in creative processes. As F. Scott Fitzgerald, an American novelist, said, "You don't write because you want to say something, you write because you have something to say." Every author in this anthology has something to say.

It is my strong belief that you will find these works to be of supreme quality. While there are certainly many anthologies containing the writings of those between the ages of 13 to 25, I believe very few, if any, have the same quality as the writings contained within. From Karina's The Magical Penguin, to Donovan's Scotch On The Rocks, you will discover a wide range of talents and genres.

So as you read and turn these pages, whether as someone who is just turning the age of 11 or as someone who is entering their retirement years, just sit back, relax and enjoy. Read for the joy of reading, and keep an eye on some of these authors. I have no doubt that one day, at least one person in this anthology will be making the New York Times bestseller list.

So with all that said, enjoy!

"Leah," an illustration by Jane H.; 16 (F) of Alaska, USA

101 TIPS FOR WRITERS
Nathaniel Lee Caldwell

The time to begin writing an article is when you have finished it to your satisfaction.
By that time you begin to clearly and logically perceive what it is you really want to say.
- Mark Twain

Whether you call yourself a young writer, a teenage writer, or just a writer, these tips are guidelines we should all follow. They apply not just to stories, but also to writing in general.

For your convenience, I have separated the 101 Tips for Writers into fifteen general topics: Set Up, Brainstorming, Pre-Writing, Beginning, While Writing, Descriptions, Characters, Dialogue, Grammar & Word Choice, Ending, Editing Process, The Review Process, The Post-Review Process, Beating Writer's Block, and General Tips. So go forth, read, and good luck!

Set Up

1. **Choose A Place:** Identify your best writing spot. Could be your room, the basement, the living room, the dog house, or, if you're really poetic, by a glistening stream.

2. **Organize:** Organize and clean your writing spot. An uncluttered room lends itself to an uncluttered mind.

3.   **Good Lighting:** Soft light? Bright light? No light? Sunlight? Lighting does make a difference, and you need to figure out which works best for you.

4.   **Temperature:** Pay attention to the temperature. Generally speaking, guys work best when the temperature is a bit colder than normal. Girls work best when the temperature is a bit warmer than normal.

5.   **Food:** Some people like to have something to nibble on when writing. Others don't. Figure out which group you belong to.

6.   **Noise:** If you prefer total silence then make sure you write somewhere silent. But if you like noise, play some music or TV.

7.   **Time:** Figure out what time of day you are in the writing zone. This will differ from person to person, and it may take a while before you figure out the perfect time of day for you.

Brainstorming

8.   **Keep A Journal:** Keeping a daily journal is the best way to keep your writing mind active.

9.   **Carry A Notepad:** Carry a notepad around with you to jot down ideas as they come to you.

10.   **Practice Writing Prompts:** Do a Google search for 'writing prompts.' Not only will these keep your writing mind engaged, but they are also a great source of ideas.

11.   **Relax:** Stress about brainstorming and your ideas will be no good. Best to relax and enjoy life. Ideas will come in good time.

12.   **Look Up Legal Cases:** Believe it or not, but legal cases are a great source of plots for stories. Go to http://www.findlaw.com/casecode and check a few.

13.   **Read:** Read, read, read! If you don't read, your mind will go to mush. If your mind goes to mush then you may as well write on napkins because that is all it will be good for.

14.   **Exercise:** You can keep your body active by just walking for thirty minutes. Keeping your body active will keep your mind active.

15.   **Study Other Writers:** When reading, don't just read, but analyze as well.

Pre-Writing

16.   **Write A Synopsis:** Write out a short one or two paragraph synopsis of the story before beginning anything else. A synopsis should be as general as possible.

17.   **Make Character Outlines:** List your main characters, and then add details even if you don't plan on using those details in the story.

18.   **Draw Scenes:** List the scenes in which your story will take place, then make simple drawings of them. Or, you can find photos of what you want your scene to look like.

19.   **Outline The Story:** Take your synopsis and add lots of detail to it. Outline in whatever fashion works for you.

20.   **Think It Over:** Before actually beginning, let the story sink into your mind for a few days.

21.   **Have Everything Ready:** Once you're almost ready to begin, make sure you have everything you need from carrots to paper.

Beginning

22.   **Do A Writing Prompt First:** You don't exercise without warming up, so why would you do differently when writing?

23.   **Relax, Let It Come:** Don't get worked up over the beginning. Your story will be the worse for it.

24.   **If In Trouble, Go For A Walk:** Walking will clear your mind.

25.   **Don't Edit, Just Write:** Push out the editor within yourself and just write. A first draft should be very rough, and you have plenty of time later to edit.

26.   **Turn On Some Background Noise:** Playing music, or just turning on something that makes noise like a fan, can help concentrate your mind on the task at hand.

27. **Start Off Generally:** Don't throw the reader into the middle of a plot. Get us introduced first.

28. **If In Trouble, Opt For A Classic Beginning:** Classic beginnings start with a description of what the character looks like, or a description of the scene. This can then build into the story.

While Writing

29. **Take Rest Breaks:** Even if you can, it is not a good idea to run a ten kilometer stretch all at once, and the same applies to writing. Take rest-breaks even when you are in the zone.

30. **Stay Awake And Alert:** If you find yourself getting tired or sleepy, stop!

31. **Don't Edit, Just Write:** Same as tip #21. If you are editing while writing, you will never complete your story.

32. **Know Your Unique Characteristics:** If you need food nearby, or if you can only write while swinging upside down from a water buffalo, know this and account for it.

Descriptions

33. **Draw Scenes:** Same as tip #18. Either drawing the scene (no matter how simplistic) or finding a photo of what you want the scene to look like will help you visualize the story.

34. **Make The Background Descriptive:** Be sure to describe the background. Doing so will draw the reader in.

35. **But Don't Over-Describe:** Just like a play only has general scenery, so should your story. Describing every plant, rock, and object will only bore your reader.

36. **Don't Use Too Many Adjectives:** Simply saying "the creaking door opened," is better than saying "the rust-ridden, brown, large rectangular door opened."

37. **Use Descriptive Verbs:** Saying "the wobbly bike" is better than saying "the bike looked like it was about to fall."

38. **Show, Don't Tell:** Saying "the wobbly bike" shows the reader that the bike is about to fall without overtly saying so.

Characters

39. **Love Your Characters, Even The Evil Ones:** If you truly love your characters, then adding depth comes naturally.

40. **Don't Be Too Cool:** No one likes a perfect character. Remember that flaws, especially of the fatal variety, are sexy.

41. **Base Your Characters On People You Know:** Basing a character on someone you know is a lot easier than making one up and you will end up with a much deeper story.

42. **Make Character Outlines:** Same as tip #17. It will be easier to explain your character's motives and histories if you outline everything about them.

43. **Give Your Character A History:** This person did not just pop out of nowhere. Give them a history showing us why we should care and why they are acting in such a manner.

44. **Ask Yourself Why:** Why is this character in the story? Why is she acting this way? Why should anyone care?

45. **How Do They Talk? Walk?:** The ways of talking and walking are unique to every person.

Dialogue

46. **Go To A Mall Or Park:** Just walking around or sitting in a very social setting will show you the different ways people talk.

47. **Listen:** Listen to what other people are saying around you and how they are talking.

48. **Have A Friend Read Out An Extended Conversation With You:** If you have a long conversation between two or more characters, then read it out loud with a group of people to make sure it makes sense and sounds right.

49.   **Nuances In Speaking:** Nobody speaks perfectly. In fact, far from it; each person has a unique way of talking.

50.   **Learn To Love Said:** Said is one of the few words a reader will automatically gloss over. Coming up with synonyms is at best unnecessary and at worse damaging to your story.

51.   **Use Quotation Marks:** Unless you are James Joyce, then use quotation marks. It does not matter if they are single or double; just be consistent.

52.   **Avoid Qualifying Said:** Be careful when you add a verb next to said, such as "quickly said" or "cautiously said." If you do your dialogue right, you won't need those extra verbs most of the time.

53.   **Know Who's Speaking:** With two characters, it is easy to tell who is speaking. But if you add more, make sure that the reader can follow who is speaking.

Grammar & Word Choice

54.   **Active Is Better Than Passive:** Using passive voice is weak and boring. Nobody says, "The theory that was formulated by Einstein." They say, "Einstein's theory."

55.   **Use Words People Know:** If you can show what the word means in the context, then good. But if you are sending your reader to the dictionary, then you are doing something wrong.

56.   **Don't Use Rarely Used Words:** There are certain rare words everyone knows, such as 'beseech' or 'arbor.' However, using a rare word will take your reader out of the story, so it is *usually* better to use common words.

57.   **Avoid Exclamation Marks:** Adding an exclamation mark is a cheap way to make something interesting and usually fails!

58.   **Avoid "Very":** Mark Twain once said, "Substitute 'damn' every time you're inclined to write 'very'; your editor will delete it and the writing will be just as it should be."

59.   **Always Toward, Never Towards. Its is not It's. Affect and Effect:** Know the differences between words, and know that words like 'towards' and 'alot' do not in fact exist.

60. **Use Spell Check, But Don't Rely On It:** Spell check is nice, but it want get al of you're miss steaks.

61. **Try To Avoid Split Infinitives:** Obviously, 'to boldly go' is better than 'to go boldly.' But if you can't make a case for using a split infinitive, then don't use it.

62. **Use A Thesaurus:** There are only a few words a reader will gloss over. Find synonyms for the others.

63. **Avoid That And This:** You should avoid that, and you should avoid this. 'That' and 'this' are not descriptive and have no place in stories.

64. ***Italics or Bold, But Not Both:*** Using italics or bold is a good way to emphasize words. But there is no need to do both.

65. **Commas At Natural Pauses:** Read, your sentence, aloud. If, a comma, makes you, stop, unnaturally then, remove, it.

66. **And Then... And Then... And Then:** If you find yourself saying 'and then' or even just 'then,' then your reader will become annoyed.

Ending

67. **Know Your Ending Before You Begin:** You shouldn't ever start a story without knowing how it will end.

68. **Stop Where The Story Ends:** Many writers want to keep writing even after the main story is over. Doing so just annoys the reader and makes the story drag on.

69. **Don't Leave The Reader Hanging... By Too Much:** Make sure you tie up all loose ends, but also make sure that you leave your reader wanting more.

70. **Leave It Alone For A While:** After you finish, leave the story alone for a few days.

Editing Process

71. **First, Revise:** After a few days pass, revision your story and ask yourself if that is how you wanted the story.

72.   **Second, Edit:** Brutalize your own work. Rework awkward sentences, ask yourself if that word is the right word, and make sure everything makes sense.

73.   **Third, Proofread:** When you proofread, you are checking your grammar. The best way to do this is to read it out loud. It can take a while, but you'll also catch a lot more miss steaks.

74.   **Show To Others:** Print out multiple copies of the story and pass it around to friends and family. They may not end up reading the whole thing, but they can still give you valuable insight.

75.   **Learn To Love The Drafting Process:** The first draft of Star Wars involved a guy named Kane Starkiller, a black knight, and Jedi Bendu. Thank God George Lucas didn't stop at a first draft.

The Review Process

76.   **Pass The Story Around:** Give your final copy to friends, family, and even literary magazines.

77.   **Put The Story Online:** Publishing your story online will give you instant access to people who actually want to read and review your work.

The Post-Review Process

78.   **Listen to Critiques:** When people critique your story, listen to them. You do not need to agree, but you should not argue either. They may be suggesting changes that would be worthwhile for you to consider.

79.   **Revisit Your Piece:** Even Star Wars isn't perfect, and George Lucas revisits it constantly. You should do the same with your story.

80.   **Makes Changes As Necessary:** If you really care about what you wrote, then you will correct mistakes and always seek to make the story better.

Beating Writer's Block

81. **Take a Break:** If you have writer's block, then step away from your story rather than trying to force it.

82. **Listen To Music:** Listening to music can help reduce stress.

83. **Take a Shower:** Showering has a cleansing effect on the body and the mind.

84. **Do Writing Prompts:** Find a few writing prompts, and do those.

85. **Don't Think About The Story:** When you get writer's block, it is best to just go and do something else that does not involve thinking about the story. The way around the block will come to you when you least expect it.

General Tips

86. **Practice:** In everything, practice makes perfect. Always write and never stop.

87. **Read:** Reading cannot be emphasized enough. In fact, all of the tips on this list mean absolutely nothing if you do not read.

88. **Pay Attention In School:** History will teach you how one event leads to another. Math will teach you how to think logically. English will teach you proper grammar.

89. **Write With Emotion. Get Enthusiastic!:** You have to like what you are writing, and you have to be enthusiastic about it. Otherwise, why are you writing?

90. **Never Give Up:** Writing is tough and grueling, but it is also rewarding.

91. **Write For Yourself:** In the end, it only matters what you think.

92. **Respect Editors:** If someone takes the time to read and review your work, then give them respect. You don't need to agree, but you don't need to tell them to shove it either.

93. **Find Your Inspiration:** Find out what motivates you to write, and then use that to keep writing.

94. **Take Your Time:** When writing a story, it's best to take it slow.

95. **Have Confidence:** Be confident about what you write. Some people will like it and others will not. That is just how the cookie crumbles.

96. **Be Prepared:** Follow the motto of the Boy Scouts and be prepared while you are writing. It is always good to have pens, pencils, paper, water, etc. nearby.

97. **Pursue Your Interests:** Do not sacrifice your hobbies and interests at the expense of writing. Writing can become a way of life, but it should not devour your life.

98. **Be A Knowledge Consumer:** Do not just read, but consume information. Read the newspaper, research random topics on Wikipedia, watch CNN.

99. **Don't Be Lazy:** There is relaxing, and then there is just being plain lazy. Just walking a mile or so can do wonders, and extracurriculars can give you valuable insight into how the world works.

100. **Be A Reporter:** A reporter always asks: Who? What? When? Where? Why? And How? You should do the same with your writing.

101. **Talent Is Cheap. Dedicated Work Is Not:** I saved the best tip for last. There are plenty of those with lots of talent, but they spend their days playing World of Warcraft or figuring out ways to do as little work as possible and get away with it. In no matter what you do, work hard and people will take notice. This applies to writing as well. If you dedicate yourself to your stories, people will take notice.

THE MAGICAL PENGUIN
Karina R.

19 (F) of California, USA

> *The magical penguin flies at night*
> *Beginning his mission of terror and fright.*
> *With his funny hat and flippery toes,*
> *Where he'll waddle off next, nobody knows!*

I'm pretty sure every workplace has It. You know what It is. That weird thing floating around the office that nobody knows exactly where It came from or even how It came into existence, or even necessarily what It is, but for some reason, probably because it was ordained by God himself, It is there.

Ours is a penguin.

It is not just any penguin -- it is the weirdest penguin you've probably ever seen. He's wearing a fez hat, he's brown in the parts that should be white, and he has a big green flower that's protruding out his chest, like some hideous cancerous growth. And he's *heavy*. That is, he looks light enough when you see him, but when you try to push him, his fired-clay body refuses to budge.

I never noticed him before the move, though I'm pretty sure he was there, lurking around the math department somewhere. He was just in the back corner, underneath several tons of dry erase markers and leftover quizzes from years past. It was only when we actually moved to the new building, that I noticed him. He was sitting off into the corner, looking slightly unloved and rather ominous, with his black wings and fez hat, just propped on his head.

I stared at him.

I'm not quite sure what surprised me about him most. Perhaps I was surprised that in a place supposed to be full of math and learning, there was some demented penguin lying around. Or maybe I was surprised because apparently he had been around for a quite a long time, and yet I only really noticed him. Whatever it was, I wasn't sure whether I should smile or try to hide the penguin again in a corner where nobody could see him.

We had a staring contest for a minute, which was only broken by the arrival of one of the math teachers. And the math teacher only broke the moment because, as all math teachers, he was carrying a stack of half-graded papers, only slightly smaller than his height. He plopped the papers on the table and muttered a hello.

I pointed to the penguin. "Where did he come from?"

The teacher did a double take.

"What?"

I gestured to the penguin. "The penguin. Do you know where it came from?" In that moment, it occurred to me how weird the scene would look. Here I was, a lowly math tutor, addressing a math teacher about a penguin with a fez hat and a big flower on its chest. In fact, come to think of it, that's probably exactly what he thought.

The teacher blinked, and concentrated so hard on the penguin that I was sure that a hole would be bored through the gaudy flower stuck to its chest. "What is *that*?"

"It's a penguin," I said.

"Yeah, but where did it come from?"

I shrugged. "I don't know."

He squinted at it for about three seconds before shrugging. "I've never seen it before," he said before changing the conversation to a completely different subject. In a couple of minutes, the poor penguin was forgotten.

And that's the way the penguin was. When the penguin was noticed, the whole world seemed to stop, but that was only when he was noticed. Otherwise, he was completely forgettable. The only person who couldn't seem to forget it was me. Whenever I leaned back in the chair and stared up into space, I would be acutely aware that somewhere in the room, underneath a black fez hat in a far corner of the room, a penguin was staring down at me.

I'm not quite sure why I first moved it. Perhaps I was delusional off math homework, tutoring, or a combination of both, but for some reason, when I walked into the staffroom in early October, one look at the penguin, shoved in the very back corner where nobody could notice it, and I knew that something had to be done about it. The question was what?

I brought it out of his corner and put it in the center table, intending to do something about it, after lunch.

Then Nathaniel came in.

Nathaniel is kind of a weirdo, but I love him for that. He has this last name that no one, not even himself, can pronounce, he has nerdy dark-rimmed glasses, and he's one of those crazy homeschoolers. Did I mention that every syllable of his is dripping with sarcasm? Because it is.

"What's that?" he asked, sitting next to me.

"It's a penguin," I said, pointing up to it. He followed my finger and then gazed it as well. "Nobody knows where it came from or anything else about it, but it's here."

"Oh." I suppose he couldn't say much to that. I fingered the penguin's wing.

"I want to put it somewhere where somebody will notice it," I said. And then, suddenly, inspiration hit me like a sack of potatoes. "I wonder," I said in an insanely fast voice, "what if we move it around the room everyday. Maybe someone will notice it!"

This got his attention. "Where would we put it?" But as soon as I opened my mouth, he had already grabbed the penguin with his superhuman strength and was lugging across the room, placing it in different poses to see where it would best fit. "Maybe we can put it on the water cooler." He almost put it on, but the water container was empty and the thing started to tip. "Not there."

"On the microwave?" I suggested. He made a face.

"I don't think he'll fit."

"He will."

"No he won't."

"Yes he will."

"No he won't."

"Yes he --"

I shall spare you the rest of the conversation, seeing as it was rather repetitious. What can I say? Nathaniel just inspires that type of profound thought. That's why he's awesome. And, for some reason, it's not even annoying participating in such a conversation with him, since he has such a good deadpan voice that it makes anything funny.

The conversation ended when I stuck my tongue at him. Which, admittedly, is a rather childish thing to do, but no more childish than the above conversation. "Wait, let's see," I said, ripping the penguin from his hands. I put him on the microwave. "See? He fits!" Nathaniel looked at him skeptically.

"Who would see him there?"

"Everybody who uses the microwave."

He moved over to the computer. "How about here?"

"If you want!"

"What about the freezer?"

"I suppose..."

And so, for the next thirty minutes, we spent our time maneuvering the penguin into different positions about the room, wondering whether the teachers would even notice. Finally, time ran out for both of us and we rushed off to tutor our math classes.

I forgot about the penguin.

And yet, the penguin seemed more alive than ever. No, I don't mean literally. But the penguin started moving everywhere. First, he was on the microwave, then he was on the table, once he was in the refrigerator, on the refrigerator, on the floor, and so on. And Nathaniel didn't move it all the time either. I know that because, even on his days off, when he didn't come to school at all, the penguin still migrated to various corners of the room.

The teachers, I think, were starting to get suspicious. When they first saw the penguin, seated upon the microwave, they raised their eyebrows and chose to ignore it. But as the penguin moved more and more, they started to look around the staffroom more, only stopping when they found the penguin.

The penguin moved many places, but it was always in the staffroom. It was only until one lunch when I came in that the penguin had disappeared entirely. I looked behind the door, in the refrigerator, the freezer, several drawers -- nothing. Confused, I decided that the penguin was probably hiding in some place I hadn't thought about and brought out my lunch, ready to heat it up.

Then, just as I set the time on the microwave, a teacher, possibly the sweetest and most decent teacher in the entire building, came out, cradling the clay penguin in her hands. She tried to smile when she saw me, an incredibly confused look on her face.

I stared at the penguin.

"Whose paperweight is this?" she said, gesturing to the penguin in her hands. When I just stared at her, she added, "I think I've seen it before, but I don't know where. I found it in my office, but it's not mine. Is it yours?" she asked, when she saw the strange look on my face.

I burst out laughing. "The penguin! He flew!"

She stared at me. Perhaps she thought I was crazy -- I don't care. I was laughing so hard that my gut ached and other teachers popped in the room, just to make sure I was all right. But, as soon as they saw the penguin on the table, now hiding in the candy dish, they smirked and turned away.

They *knew* what was happening.

The penguin returned to us for a short time in the staffroom after that incident, but he has since disappeared. Trust me, I've looked everywhere for him, and yet I have not found him or his strange hat and flippery toes. Nor do any of the teachers or tutors know where he is -- I've asked.

I have theories, mind you. He may be hiding in the layers of dusty math quizzes hidden in the testing room. Or perhaps he is residing with one of the teachers, hiding off into the corner, ready to strike. I can only guess where he could be, but I am confident that one day, hopefully in the near future, he will pop out and once more bring mystery and laughter into our lives.

Until then, watch out for the magical penguin in your own neighborhood. Who knows? He might appear in your freezer and jump out when you least expect it. You never know with a magical penguin...

LOVE SONG
Via M.

19 (F) of Ohio, USA

As I stepped out of the cabin, the morning sun peered over the horizon to my right. I pulled my jacket closed a little more as the cold air nipped at my nose. Turning my head to shield my face from the wind, I caught a glimpse of my twenty-foot long shadow atop a thin layer of snow. "Let's go for a walk" I demanded, for it's not like he had a choice. We made our way into the wooded hills and chose a trail to follow. The new snow glimmered on the trees like a diamond on the finger of a new bride-the first snow of the season. In the distance, rushing water could be heard. A sudden vision of a waterfall in the dead of winter came over me. We, my shadow and I, turned towards the water. We walked and walked and walked-the sound began to echo but the origin had yet to be discovered. "Why don't *you* take the feet for awhile?!" I said to my shadow, for it seemed we were in a different dimension from the brook. "This is a water of time, all this walking to get nowhere. Might as well be sleeping," I stated…both took so much time out of the day yet accomplished nothing. And even if we did find it, we'd just have to turn around and walk all the way back again-like making the bed when you're just going to sleep in it again anyway—pointless. Pointless time spent doing nothing when you could be out discovering a cure for cancer or winning a noble prize. Time that could have been spent with family and friends—that *I* could have spent with family and friends.

Just to travel the country with him again—the Grand Canyon, Mount Rushmore, Yellowstone. Or to see him steer that boat again…or to sit on his lap and pretend not to be ticklish one last time.

But I suppose some would spend the time pretending to be invincible while bungee jumping from impossible heights…or jumping out of planes…or street racing. Tomorrow is guaranteed like acing a paper-you can never really be certain it will happen. "We were going to tell you tomorrow," he said, his emerald hues reflecting the light of the moon. Glancing around you realize everyone knew but you, and you suddenly feel like an ant under a magnifying glass. His perfect smile so deceiving—knowing he was screaming inside.

A single drop of water fell from a tree and landed on my nose, snapping me back into reality. I turned to my shadow to make sure he was still there, as if he could leave. Continuing, we came to one lone tree in the middle of the pathway. "I wonder if he's lonely there by himself," I said, more to myself than to anyone, or any*thing*, else. There are so many other trees everywhere but he chose to grow there—all by his lonesome. Just then a squirrel ran down the tree trunk, across the trail and up another tree—out of sight, like a bolt of lightening. But not the kind of lightening that comes from a big storm—more peaceful than that. More like the heat lightening that can be admired from a front porch as it brightens up the country sky on a hot summer night. The kind that makes you feel so at ease that if death were to personally walk up to you and stare you in the face, you wouldn't care. But, like the lightening, those moments quickly pass and you are thrown back into the real world. You come to realize, however, just one of those moments a month makes everything in your life seem worth while—so you stay strong and stick it out, trying to be as noble as Aslan. For when silver locks fall down your back and your skin wrinkles, the only thing that will matter will be experiences you had that made you smile. It won't matter if you never became rich and lived in a mansion with your seven kids and your twelve maids—most of us will never experience that.

And then finally—the brook.

GEEK

Samantha R.

19 (F) of Northants, England
I might not even be
A pixel on their bitmap
I'm just a tag-along icon,
Or a hovering cursor.
But tell me it really doesn't matter-
The only thoughts of importance are yours.

Edit undo, edit redo,
Nothing that I do
Would interest your friends
And most of mine got lost
During a system restore.

ALONE AGAIN
Abbey M.

15 (F) of Arizona, USA

Alone again.

I wish I had seen it coming. Maybe I had just misread your signs. They were all there. Now I'm sitting alone in our favourite café, the bright orange wallpaper falling dead on my dark coloured eyes. My hand is burning from the coffee cup I clench tightly like a last lifeline to a dying man, but I hardly notice.

You're just never there, Jack.

Your words still ring in my ears, as if there's a minute gramophone in my ear that's skipping.

A relationship has to go two ways.

I understand.

I don't think you do, Jack.

I do now.

The pain of the reality hits me like a blow to the head with a nine iron golf club. I zip up my fluffy black jacket, tug my gloves and knit wool cap on, and exit the café; diving headlong into the raging blizzard outside. My coffee lies long forgotten on the table, alongside the one you abandoned. They sit at the table like lovers who have forgotten what love is. I turn my head away as I plow through the storm.

I can see you standing, shivering at the bus stop just a few feet down the road. I decide my actions on impulse and hurry up behind you, my face already numb and red in the viciously cold wind.

"Riley," I say. You turn.

"Jack," you say. I try to move closer to you, but you step away like I'm carrying some infectious disease that you don't want to catch. "Jack, don't try to make up for it now."

"I'm not," I say, but of course you don't believe me. I don't believe myself, either. A bus pulls up behind you, its roar drowning any words that would have filled in that moment. The smell of the cloud of exhaust still burns my nostrils, imprinted forever on my memory, just like your face that day.

You shiver in the cold, your dark hair flying all over, tossed by the freezing wind. Your eyes, your beautiful blue eyes are unusually cold and sad, like the weather. All too like the weather. I want to wrap my arms tightly around you, share our body heat so the blizzard seems less vicious, so that the wind will die down somehow, so you smile again like you did so long ago. It pains me to see you this sad, but you speak with a solid confidence, that feisty determination of yours that I foolishly fell in love with, and I know I cannot change your mind. I'm beating a dead horse. I know it. I can't stop myself.

I love you.

Did those words ever really mean anything?

"Jack, I really do like you," you say in an irritatingly patronising tone after the noise from the retreating bus fades away. "But I feel like you never pay attention to me, or anything else for that matter. You were always off in your own little world, so far removed from me, lost in those damn stories of yours. You love your characters more than you ever loved me, and what do you think it feels like to be less important than a fictitious being? You were there physically but never mentally, Jack. I need more than just a warm body at my side. I need a warm heart and a mind that's all there, and there for me when I need it."

I nod, my blond hair falling in the way of my face. I hope you don't see what I'm feeling through my eyes. It would just overcomplicate things. The ensuing silence is awkward, stretching on for days in the space of a few moments. I feel your eyes on me and I sense something strange. Is it pity? Remorse? Dare I think it... love?

"Goodbye, Jack," you say.

"Riley, please don't go, I need you," I say, reaching out for your arm, hopeless even as I do so. This seems to anger you. I can feel it even before you say it.

"Jack, you are so selfish," you say impatiently. "You're too busy moping about to care that maybe you're not what I want; but of course not, it's all about Jack, it's all about your feelings, never mine. You want me to stay, and for what reason? Face value? A pretty bracelet? A girl toy? Nuh-uh, Jack, never.

You know how I feel about that. And if there's any other reason you want me to stay, go ahead and tell me, because it'll be news to me."

You stand with one hand on your hip, staring me down. I say nothing; I don't need to. The beauty is in what isn't said. Your mind is made up. As much as I'd like to, there's no way in thirteen lifetimes that I'd be able to change it. Your resolve is too strong.

"I thought so," you say, icicles dripping off your voice. "You know what, Jack, stay away from me. I never want to see you again. Stay away from everything that involves me. I don't want you at my college graduation, at my wedding, even at my funeral. Even if we meet on the street I don't want to see you. Cross the street and look the other way. Thanks for the coffees and the one or two laughs on the rare moments I had your mind with me. Goodbye, Jack. I wish you bad luck, good luck, and everything in between."

You huff at me and march across the street in anger, seeming to forget where you are. I don't have the time to stop you, to bring you back to earth. You are just as far gone as I am.

I see the bus come in slow motion, like those drama films we used to hold so dear. My mind somehow deleted the segment in between when you walked off and when the people started screaming, their cries shattering the winter air. I'm actually thankful for that; it's not something I want haunting my memories.

I honour your final wish and walk away, my feet carrying my wandering mind to our flat- now just mine-, leaving the scene of bloody death behind.

Alone again.

SETTING UP REBECCA
Danielle G.

21 (F) of Colorado, USA

There is a kind of oppressive giddiness when something new enters your life. The giddiness comes from the unexpectedness of the thing, which seems to pop out of nowhere and the oppressiveness happens when you fail to control these new emotions and they inexplicably seem to take over your life. This was exactly what happened to Rebecca, who found that this phenomenon usually occurred when she was clearly not in her right mind, but that mostly, this curious and sometimes troubling sate of being transpired because that something new in her life was another person. For Rebecca, that person happened to be the hottest thing since sliced bread, and James, she was sure, was sliced, ripped and any other synonym for the word chiseled found in the English dictionary.

They had met-

What does it matter where they had met? Just skip to the kissing bit will you?!

I'll get there in a moment, Rebecca, patience.

Uhg!

They had met in the most awkward and dreaded of all social situations; a wedding. Not just any wedding. It was her 2nd cousin, Mary's wedding. Mary was a sorority bimbo whose main joy in life was creating marital "happiness" for any of her single friends she could get her lotiony hands on. She had been working on Rebecca for years and wasn't about to give up yet.

But I won't fall for her tricks, no matter how many drinks I've had.

Alas, Rebecca had underestimated Mary's desperation to see all her girlfriends, including her cousins, settled with a man (despite some of their differing orientations) and that evening, during the reception, before the happily wedded couple flew off to Paris or Pompeii or wherever overly wealthy people usually honeymooned, Mary had arranged for Rebecca and Mr. James E. Ferris to find themselves alone and, from Rebecca's standpoint, under the worst circumstances.

I'll say.

"You had better take her upstairs James," Mary cooed, unable to hide her malicious delight at her cousin's drunken stupor. "She really doesn't look very well. I just don't know how she managed to drink *all* that champagne."

"I'll take care of her, Mary. Don't worry."

And the next thing Rebecca knew, she was hauled to the master bathroom by a pair of well-muscled arms-

God they were beautiful arms-

and strong hands that gently held back her hair; though she would admit later to a lapse in memory when it came time to recall that bit of the night. Still, with some help, she made it to her date with the toilet just in time.

"Are you, all right?" he asked her, unsure about whether that was too obvious a question or not. She stumbled toward the bed and tripped over a chair. He caught her.

"Thanks. I'm sorry about all this. You shouldn't have to take care of me."

"It's not a problem." He brought her upright and held her steady.

"It's just-"

"I know. Mary. She thinks she can just throw two people together and they'll live happily ever after. Let's just get you in bed."

"Excuse me?" she scoffed, with a slight slur.

Rebecca was short.

Too Short.

Yes, too short. At least, too short in the way that she could never play basketball-   *Not well, anyway.*

-and that one item on the top shelf, which she could have reached were she a mere two inches taller, always alluded her. *Damn canned soup aisle.* Her height had always bothered her. It was that one thing. Everyone has that one thing.

Yeah, but most people can tone their butts or pay for breast implants. How many people do you know who can male themselves grow?

Actually, there is a very interesting theory that states-

Does this really have anything to do with my story?

Ah. Well, no.

Just get on with it.

So, Rebecca was short and had struggled with this vertical challenge for a very long time, however, being a person of small stature and large personality, she naturally, had a desire to learn to defend herself at a very young age and by the time she was fourteen had advanced to her second black belt, in Kim Li's Karate class. It was perhaps, because of this, and her inebriated state of mind, that when James answered her reply with-

"I need to get you on the bed."

- she instinctively jabbed him in the chest with her elbow, grabbed his arm and flung him over her shoulder onto the floor. A moment after, when she had realized that he had actually meant to help get her to sleep, she was on the floor next to him and apologizing in a way that would make even Antony forgive Cleopatra, had they had the chance to talk before committing suicide.

"Are you ok? I'm so sorry." She prayed she hadn't broken anything.

"Yeah, no, I'm fine," he moaned and then looked up at her and smiled. "Wow, you really took me down!"

She gave him a slight, and because she was still drunk, sloppy, grin when he got to his feet.

"I guess I just didn't realize what you," she clutched her stomach, feeling nauseous again. "Oh, god, I think I need to puke again."

Now, normally one would think a person who, when confronted with the terrible fate of hanging her head over a toilet seat and expelling what was left of her dinner, right down to the Cheeseit's she had eaten before the wedding, would not be looking for love and would not think this, of all moments, would be a moment for true love to appear. This is exactly what Rebecca was not thinking, but the thought did, briefly, wander into James' mind as he pulled the fuchsia and flower patterned bed spread over Rebecca's shoulders.

The phone rang!

Ahh!

Was it him? Could it possibly be?

Of course it's him. Ok, be cool, calm down!

Two days later, James E. Ferris had tracked down her number and asked her to accompany him to a dinner party. The event itself had been a complete disaster.

You're telling me.

James' friends, like him, were theatre people. Not the kind of theatre people who reveled in the dull avant-garde, modern art world, but the type who, by age twelve had memorized every song in "Singin' in the Rain" and all the choreography to "Thriller".

Their night went something like this. The hostess of the party could not keep her hands off James and spent the entire evening interrupting him, asking him to help her amuse her guests, while James' only goal was to entertain and converse with Rebecca, who in turn was pestered by a very eccentric, older man who related his entire life story to her through the context of his extensive porcelain cat collection.

I don't think I'll ever recover from that.

Afterwards, the two agreed that their date, though disastrous and unconventional, may have actually benefited from their friends' unwanted interruptions.

And now he had called her. They had gone out five times in the last three weeks and she –

Who cares! He's calling. Tell them about when he calls!

– she had not been expecting his call this evening and was rather surprised when his name showed up on her cell phone.

"Hello."

"Hey, how you doing?"

"I'm doing well, what are you up to?" Her heart thumped. Loudly.

"Gonna be in your part of town tonight, thought I'd see if you wanted to go out?"

Yes, of course yes.

She wanted to go out with him, but knew she had a prior engagement.

"I would love to, but I've already promised my aunt I would spend the evening with her. What time were you going to be over?"

"Later. Thought I might hang out with my friend Michelle; maybe watch a movie."

Michelle!?

Her heart pounded louder with unexpectedness.

"She asked me to bring you along," he continued. "She wants to meet you."

"That sounds fun," she lied, trying to hide her real feelings about the situation. "But I really can't cancel on my aunt. I'll see if I can get back early. Where does she live?"

She arrived at Michelle's house at 9:15 that evening. Her aunt had a meeting the next morning she needed to prep for.

More like her husband was away for the weekend and she wanted alone time in her King size bed.

This meant Rebecca had left straight after dinner. She stood on Michelle's doorstep, feeling quite apprehensive. She wasn't sure what to do. Should she knock?

Why am I even here? What if this "Michelle" girl isn't just his friend?

She decided to knock. There was no answer.

Great.

She knocked again.

"Hey!" It was him, smiling, obviously glad to see her.

"Hi." She stepped inside.

"Michelle! Rebecca's here!" he yelled out to the porch. "Michelle's great. I think you'll like her a lot."

"Yeah."

"Want a beer?"

'Sure, why not."

"We're hanging out outside. The back porch is straight through there." He pointed towards a door at the end of the living room. "See you in a minute." He smiled and she felt like melting.

Her journey to the porch was not a pleasant one. She moved through the small dinning room and next into the living room, where the door to the outside was. She felt strange, as though moving through peanut butter, only without the sticky factor. Her thoughts raced many miles per hour. Was Michelle pretty? Prettier than her? Maybe she should have touched up her hair.

My hair is fine.

What if this Michelle didn't like her?

Does it matter?

What if Michelle told James she didn't like her and then James decided to stop seeing her? Or worse.

That's impossible.

Is it? *Yes, it is. I think.*

Rebecca turned the knob, slowly opened the back door and stepped out onto the porch.

"Hi. She muttered."

"Hey! Rebecca right?"

She was larger than Rebecca-

Duh, most people are!

-not enormous, but you could tell that she enjoyed her double bacon cheeseburger once and a while and with little exercise afterwards. A small, red headed two year old wriggled on her lap, grasping a sippy cup. For a moment, Rebecca breathed in a sigh. She was safe. But, wait.

No, oh no!

She began to do what she always did in uncertain situations; she assumed the worse. Whose child was this, if not theirs? James had not told her everything, yet. She felt the girl must be his. She had no other explanation.

"That's me. You're Michelle?" she guessed. It must be her since there was no one else around.

"And this is Alice."

"Hi Alice."

"Pri-dy dress."

"Thank you, I like yours too."

"So…"

And comes the interrogation.

What? No!

"Where are you from Rebecca?"

Phew! As long as it's not about James and me. I'm just not ready for that.

I know, Rebecca.

Of course you know. You know more than I do.

I am the one telling this story, aren't I?

Sorry, please continue.

Thank you. Rebecca answered Michelle's inquiry, grateful to not have to talk about her and James or Michelle and James for that matter.

"I grew up in Maryland, but my parents live in Colorado now. I'm just out here visiting my grandparents and looking for work."

Mostly, this was all true, but Rebecca had left out one very large detail. She had come to California for her cousin's wedding and to interview for an internship on a movie set, which she had later discovered wasn't for her-

Damn Hollywood people!-

and once the wedding was over, she was supposed to have left. Instead, she had let her feelings get the better of her.

Again.

She felt there was truly something special between her and James and was determined to find out if that feeling was real or not.

James reappeared.

At last.

He smiled at her and handed her a Stella, one of her favourites. His smiles tended to cause the all the muscles in her body to tremble.

"Having a good time?" He sat in a chair and picked up the acoustic that sat next to it. He began to play.

"Yeah," said Michelle. "just asking Rebecca here how she puts up with you playing those damn twelve songs over and over again." James gave her a look that said, you know you love my songs, and went back to playing.

"Actually, this is the first time I've heard him play."

" Really? Well. Maybe you can inspire him to write some new ones." Rebecca giggled. Michelle was funny, at least.

"I'll see what I can do," she promised. She walked over to sit next to James and placed a hand on his knee. Alice looked up from her sippy cup and stared blankly at Rebecca for a couple moments and then with great intensity, as though unsure what to think about this new stranger in her home. Rebecca stared back, looking for some sign of James in those light blue eyes. Alice must have decided Rebecca was worthy of her time, for a moment later she posed a command.

"Play game," she demanded of Rebecca.

"Uh, sure."

The little munchkin hopped off her mother's lap and headed into the yard. Rebecca followed; unaware that this was the first of many play dates with little Alice. She looked back at James, as Alice led her to a sand box. He made a face and winked at her. She smiled.

Yes!

RIVER OF PROBLEMS
Alex W.

17 (M) of Florida, USA

Bleeding from the earth's muddy skin is an unclogging cut

Which trees and shrubs make half-efforts to close

Only while the foreman makes his rounds.

How does a rushing force drag such serenity behind it?

Animals from all walks of life come to watch

As wraiths of another time constantly push water downstream

Filling a sieve with sand

Never grumbling, never pausing, forever forward moving.

The blood overflows with spectres and their partners.

Still the incision remains

Propelling its children into the depths of the canyon

Groping in the blinding darkness for a glimmer that does not soon come

While mother sits content, spouting words of encouragement

With deceit oozing between her teeth.

Perhaps the problem is buried below this patch of disturbed dirt:

The river remains in motion, yet it never moves.

Liberating the branches of a tree does nothing to topple it

When the fingers return before the limbs strike the ground.

So on rushes the roaring water from an unrelenting heart
As yesterday's ghosts facilitate its flow
With arms cursed to an eternity of labor
And feet too sluggish to outpace
An unsolvable riddle.

STRANDS OF DARKNESS
Omar S.

18 (M) of New South Wales, Australia

Phyllis Brook bumbled about within a nest of charts and diagrams. He was never still, filled with a frenetic energy that propelled him all about his small shop. Maps, in all their wondrous variety, covered the walls. Beautiful, antique, hand drawn maps; exquisitely detailed, lovingly made examples of a burning obsession.

The bell above the door tinkled, freezing the old man mid-step. His head whipped around, pinning the unfortunate boy with his gaze. It was hard to say who was more surprised: the man, at being interrupted, or the boy, confronted by a little old man with electric blue eyes and a head of messy white hair.

The stalemate lasted a few moments more before the boy nodded at him, breaking the spell, and entering the shop. He was an oddly serious child, the mapmaker could see, dressed in a maroon and grey school uniform. He glanced around, fascinated by all the maps.

Phyllis smiled. "Hello there, young man. What can I do for you?" He wrung his hands. His loose, dry skin shriveled with each passing caress, liver spots rolling.

"I'm meant to be doing an assignment for school," the boy said, by way of explanation. "On maps," he added.

The old man beamed. "Well then you've come to the right place, lad, yes indeed! Oho!" He was all but clapping with glee. "The name is Phyllis," he said, shaking the young boy's hand. His hand lingered. He turned away, back to the recesses of the room.

"My name is Tim, sir," the boy said to Phyllis' retreating back. He thought nothing of the old man's reticence, more interested in what the shop had to offer. He walked over to the wall on the right, where a large map was hung like a tapestry. Hills, trees, mountains, individual cottages were all shown in detail.

The material was aged with fine cracks, but was still soft to the touch. It felt familiar somehow. Above the plains, in large fancy writing it said: Lyceum. He frowned. He hadn't ever heard of such a country. He turned to the next one. It seemed to be of the local town. So intent was he on the map, that Phyllis' approach went unnoticed.

"I have maps of every country and every world," Phyllis whispered in Tim's ear.

The boy jumped, a small scream escaping his throat.

The old man blinked, surprised. "Did I scare you?" he asked, head tilted. His blue eyes were hard, predatory.

Tim hesitated. There was something odd in the man's voice. Mouth dry, he nodded. Phyllis shuddered.

"I made them all, you know," he said, running a gentle hand over the nearest. A faint smile lingered on his lips.

"I-I- really like this one," Tim said, pointing to Lyceum. "It feels funny though."

Phyllis stared at the boy, eyes half lidded. For the first time, he stood completely still, seeming to gather himself. "You can see that, can you?" he asked, licking dry lips. Puzzled, Tim nodded, wondering if he'd said the wrong thing. Phyllis placed the book he had retrieved on a cluttered table nearby.

"Not many people can see the truth," he said, walking to the door. He locked it, turning back to face the school boy. "Such individuals are... *unique.*"

"Why did you lock the door?"

Phyllis came over toward the child, kneeling so they were face to face. He smiled at the boy's fear. "Lyceum is a far off place, lad, a much distant world," he said, ignoring the question. "And the material this map is made from, ah, it is a fine thing indeed. It lasts the longest, as you can see, but alas, its usage has long since faded in this realm of men... till now." He grinned, revealing sharp teeth that gleamed.

When had it gotten so dark? "I want to go home now," Tim said, backing away.

"I'm afraid it's too late for that, Timmy," Phyllis said, herding the boy calmly into the back room. "I specialise in unique maps you see."

Tim stumbled, crashing to the ground behind the counter. He got the man's meaning well enough. "What are you doing?" he squeaked.

Phyllis smiled. "Every little line on your face, every scar and mole," he reached out, running a hand lightly over the boy's face. "Tells a story; your skin becomes a map of your life. And I am the Map Maker." A silver gleam in his other hand drew Tim's eye. He screamed as the knife flashed toward him.

Crooning softly, he dragged the body into the back and set to work.

Part II

People often misconstrue the beauty of the blank canvas. They see it as nothing, something merely to support the vision. Ivan knew better though, gazing into the pristine surface, waiting. He sat on a small crotchety stool, placed before the open double window, staring at the canvas in anticipation. Through the window streamed the noise of the busy metropolis, the chatter, laughter, yelling … the *stench* of humanity, tinged by the hues of a crimson gold sunset. He let it flow over him and into his cramped apartment undisturbed.

He so rarely ventured out anymore, that it was a blessing merely to feel the heat of the sun on his skin. He knew what people said about his absence, heard the whispers that surrounded him; naming him obsessed, eccentric, mad. He didn't care about the jealous slander; art was all he had. His passion, his love was being abused, and he had to fix it. No longer did the visionaries bless the grey world with their presence.

The truth, the secret, lay in the blood.

He sat for days, merely waiting. Some pictures were harder to coax forth. This one took three days; rough stubble shadowed his delicate features and a haunted look grew in eyes stressed and red from avid search. Exhausted, he smiled suddenly, then leaned forward, nub of a pencil in multi-hued fingers and began to draw. It always gave him a rush, the feeling of creating, of power; a brush with divinity that made him ache for more. The first bold stroke, the dark outlining shapes, things previously hidden.

He could see it now: a street encrusted in filth. Against a blur of people walking by a road oozing black blood along exposed veins, there existed a miracle of nature—a puddle in a pothole. The dark rain water pooled, glacial and still, nursing in its centre, a perfect flower. Brilliant red petals fanned outward, a contrast so vivid it seemed to leak into the water, while in the centre a soft gold shone.

It was lovely. And yet, something was wrong. His head was pounding, his vision swam and the image flickered. Ivan was confused; this had never happened before. Always his genius would spread unhindered across the canvas. Unnoticed, blood dripped from his nose, falling silently on the floorboards. Instead of the perceived pothole, a very different image was shaping up beneath his hand—a backdrop of mountains, rising spires, trees. He shook his head, trying to clear it; blood splattered onto the canvas.

He raised a shaking hand, only now aware of the blood streaming from his nose. His breaths were rapid and short, pupils dilated. He flushed, a wave of heat rising up from the floor to his head. All the while his hands jerked and flashed erratically over the page with a will of their own and a sinister world came to life. He could see the few trees he'd individualized from the forest, sway in a breeze. He felt his body go slack and lean in, drawn closer. His head flew backward and a massive sneeze rocked his body, spraying the art with blood, freeing him from its grasp. His mind was numb with shock, mouth agape in silent terror. But he couldn't stop. The painting had to be finished.

Night descended on the outside world and cold stars glared down on the city. The hectic rush of man and machine slowed as lights and nylon signs burst into life. Ivan reached to the side, losing the pencil and acquiring a small, fine brush. He began to gently but firmly apply pressure, smearing his blood into a light haze. The painter in him knew this shouldn't be possible, was aware that normally the blood would dry and be difficult to spread. It was as if the laws of reality had been suspended just for the unfolding of this... nightmare.

After many hours Ivan stood back, exhausted and still. He felt not the usual triumph, but a hollow emptiness. Never had he created something so powerful, so dark that it tugged at his soul even as he watched. Vaguely, he was aware of a gnawing horror. When one paints a vision, a world, he gives away a part of himself; the art is a reflection of innermost self. But this, Ivan knew, was not one such. It had nothing to do with him. "This is no' right," he said aloud. Behind him, a voice answered: "But it is beautiful nonetheless."

Ivan whirled, heart pounding. Standing there was a tall man, richly dressed in black velvet. Swaying on his feet, Ivan could only get an impression: of dark sable hair, intense silver eyes, a trim salt and pepper goatee. The man reached out a hand. "And so are you," he finished, gently cupping the surprised artist's chin. Before he could do anything but gape, the man raised an ebony cane and smashed it across Ivan's face.

The force of the blow sent Ivan reeling, spinning him backward and onto the painting. Yet he felt no resistance, and continued to fall. The man watched, impassive, but silently regretful as Ivan began screaming. The painting sucked and tore at him; pulling him in. Just as suddenly as it had begun, the screaming stopped and Ivan was gone. The painting remained, gleaming now with a polished coat.

The man stepped forward, stroking the map that had brought him here. He studied the painting for a moment, as sounds of music and people drifted in on the ghost of a breeze. "Your blood is your cage. My collection is mine," he said ritually, as he'd done, for the past hundred years. "And you are the last, the final piece."

Part III

The hiss and crackle of static filled the room. The blue glow of the television illuminated the couch and the bedraggled form of the boy sleeping on it. He shifted slightly, weight pressing down on the remote. Immediately the static vanished, replaced with a current affairs program and the crisp, clear tones of a news reader could be heard:

'Good morning, and welcome to this urgent report. Today, police confirmed that another person has gone missing, the latest of a series of bizarre missing person cases that have left authorities baffled. Simon Green, 16, is only the most recent of what began with the case of little Timothy Roberts...'

Paul Brook awoke. He stared blearily at the screen for a moment, confused, before leaping forward in alarm.

"Shit, what time is it?" he muttered. He cast about for his phone, finding it wedged between cushions, and cursed as he discovered he was late for school. He had just begun his senior year at Plenetary High. Constantly late, forever dreamy, he was the prime target of many a teacher's lecture. Not that it had any effect. He ran a hand roughly through his messy locks, hoisted his bag, and left for school with a sigh.

The day passed in a blur of shouting faces, mumbled apologies and heart-felt groans. As he walked away from yet another lecture, toward the end of the day, Paul wondered why he even bothered. He was sure that if it weren't for his friends, he'd have left a long time ago. Well, that and his mother. She had cancer. Every day he had to face her painfully thin figure, and those too bright eyes that gleamed with hope when she saw him. He couldn't bear to dash that hope, and so everyday continued the charade.

'How are things at school, honey?' she asked.

He forced himself to look into her eyes, and lie. 'It's going great mum, really.'

A wistful smile twisted her lips and she turned away, so he didn't notice the tears slide down her face. He stared at the white hand clutching the hospital sheets, and tried to imagine they were at home and everything was okay. It never worked.

Paul shook himself, trying to think of better things. He didn't want to brood today. The final bell rung and with a clatter and scrape of moving chairs, everyone packed up and left. Paul was slower to his feet today, even though normally he'd be the first out the door. He didn't feel well today. As he left the school grounds, he was joined by best friend, Nick. Immediately the mood changed, and within moments they were laughing and chattering. Nick had that effect on people. Good looking, with dark hair and blue eyes, he was an athletic freak and resident popular kid.

They moved within the stream of students heading toward the station; a great migration of exuberant youth. It was Friday and they had every reason to be excited. They had happy, healthy families to rush home and greet. Thinking of this, Paul felt the happiness bleed away from him, and saw the same effect occur on Nick's face.

'What's up, mate?'

'Nothing, just thinking of my mum.'

'Ah.' Nick shifted, uncomfortable.

At that moment, Paul hated himself. Who was he to spoil another's day? With an effort, he pushed the dark thoughts away, and concentrated on being happy. Or what passed for it anyway. After a while, the tension eased and they talked good naturedly of the footy and upcoming assessments. At a cross-road, Paul led his friend away from the rest and headed toward the library. It wasn't far away, and they had research to do after all.

It was a strange, murky day. The type everyone hated. Brooding grey clouds smothered the light, but still the heat was stifling. Speeding motorists steadily chugged out polluting fumes, making them cough and splutter as they crossed the street. Again, silence stretched between them.

'So, what's going on with you and Samantha?' Paul asked, desperate to start the conversation again.

'Huh? I—we—what are you... how the hell did you know?' he finally protested.

Paul couldn't help but laugh at the wounded puppy look Nick was giving him. As if he'd thought he'd done a great job of hiding his new found romance.

'Oh, you know, I have my ways,' Paul said airily.

In truth Nick had been strutting around the grounds all week, chest puffed out and proud, like a prize winning peacock. Paul wasn't about to mention that though.

Up ahead a cluster of buildings huddled together, as if afraid. Gradually, they crept closer, looming above the boys. A biting cold wind cut into them, slicing through the meagre protection afforded by their clothes. Big, fat droplets of rain began to fall, smacking into them, at first singly then in torrents. Breathless and drenched, they skidded to a halt in front of the library entrance. The automatic doors slid open. The shadowed interior beckoned. Nick looked back at him.

'Come on already, I need to go to the toilet.'

'And what? You need me to hold your hand?' Paul snorted, but followed him anyway. He needed to go as well.

They approached the toilets. There was movement in the upper levels, but nothing distinct. Again, Paul was struck with an odd feeling. Irritable, he pushed open the door and was instantly bathed in harsh UV light. Smooth, gleaming white tiles covered the floor, reflecting the light as waves. Rows of cubicles stretched away. Within one of them, someone was whistling.

Despite being the one to bring them here, Nick didn't go to the toilet. Instead, he approached the mirrors, and stood there adjusting his hair. Paul made a noise of disgust and found himself a cubicle. He relieved himself, listening to the whistler. It was an odd tune, and one Paul felt he ought to remember. At the same time he felt his stomach clench, sickened, as a thick metallic taste flooded his mouth.

Somewhere further down, a door creaked open.

Despite this, no footsteps could be heard. It was the song that approached, dark, swelling with ugly promise. Everything in Paul screamed at him to run, to hide and cower; trembling, he resisted. It sliced into his gut, penetrating his roiling insides, coiling there, serpentine. He dry heaved, hunched over. It was under his skin, crawling, invading, and probing sharply. It lanced into his eyes. It was, he realized, searching him. Two, glossy dark shoes halted outside his cubicle. Paul felt his heart lurch. Sweat dripped down his face.

After a moment, the shoes slid on. Suddenly the pain was gone, and Paul sucked in air gratefully, shaking with relief. He knew he should call out, give warning, scream—But he didn't, paralysed by fear. He heard a brief scuffle, a muffled shout, and then nothing. The tune continued, triumphant, and full.

He was vaguely aware of opening the door, of rushing to the piles of clothing and empty bag of skin and bones that were all that remained of his best friend. Then he remembered screams, terrible gut wrenching wails of horror and flashing blue and red lights. He was numb to it all. He heard only the song.

A comforting blanket was placed about his shoulders and he was led away, a strong authoritarian voice assuring him everything would be okay. He was placed in a police car and driven away. Hours passed. He stared blankly out the window, and only after a long while had passed, was he aware of what he stared at. Long swathes of desert greeted his eye. He frowned.

'Hello?' he said. Or tried to anyway. All that emerged was a strangled croak. The cop said nothing. Licking his lips he tried again.

'Hello? Officer?'

Nothing.

'Sir? Hello? Where are you taking me?'

Silence was the only answer he received. The car raced on, hurtling away from everything he knew. He began to breathe heavily, panic setting in.

'Help me!' he screamed. He thrashed. He pleaded and begged but heard nothing in reply. After a while, the officer began to whistle.

THE VOICES
Clair N.

15 (F) of Arizona, USA

The voices were back, hauntingly familiar. They always returned—sometimes after a long drink of something warm and cozy, sometimes after the feel of soft fur between coarse fingers. They always found a way to reach out to Ingrid, using their icy fingers and manipulating rhythm, ensnaring her within their firm grasp.

They spoke, not always in English, as if narrating a story already told. They knew the beginning, they sensed the present, and they foreshadowed the dreadful ending. They knew how she would die, how her last breaths would escape her throat like so many droplets of blood.

She would face her fate with a cold reality and indifference, just to prevent her from giving the voices any satisfaction. She would not give them even that.

They already took more than she could possible give. It seemed that every moment she spent breathing, awake, staring at her ceiling or at the sweaty palms of her hands, was with the voices. They were loud at times, screaming with indignant pride and unrelenting effort, and were so muffled and quiet at other times, that they were more like butterfly wings brushing softly against the fabrics of her mind.

The words were not always completely audible, and not always understandable. Some sentences could not be distinguished from others, and when they could they usually came with foul language and heavy perspiration. Ingrid tried to write them down when she could, believing with an intangible hope that if all the words were visible, perhaps they would make a shred of sense.

Backward glances....of proprietary...

Ingrid's pen scratched the paper on her desk with an affirmative that made her insides squelch. Thousands of crumpled pieces of paper lay beside her, forming a mountain that bellowed, "Failure, failure, FAILURE!"

She would not fail this time. *Drawing on the brink of....reality in the midst of....mist....mixed...*

Her mind could not focus in the sweltering heat. God, it was so hot, so hot! The windows were open, the door was open, and the walls were falling away, but the heat, the heat! She couldn't stand it, the salt, the tears, the sweat, the salt, all mixing together in pools of sticky liquid at her feet. She couldn't, she mustn't.....she had to....

Drawing on the brink of reality...in the midst of immortality...and unaffectionate...

Too much air, too much air...she was suffocating in the openness, the bright light, it blinding the very core of her existence...if she could only get out, get free! If there could only be one goddamn breeze in the whole city...but they would not give her that, would they? They would torture, here, in her mind and in her soul, her spirit in the pen, writing, writing, forever writing, of nothing, of everything, of herself and of them...embedding them in the ink that dripped like so much blood...

They would not let her escape.

They would not let her escape.

SINCE FOREVER
Milly A.

13 (F) of UK

A tear falls, to die on my shoulder,
The first of many tonight
As I lie, motionless,
Under the stars that have become my home.

You gave me the power to fly,
So I soared over constellations,
Walked on clouds, dived,
Fell, inside, knowing it couldn't last.

And every kiss, every step, every word
I savoured, knowing it may be the last.
But the final kiss would not be as sweet, the
Step as light, the word as soft as this.

Yet here I am, alone. Watching, waiting
For you. Although I know you will never return.
As I stand on this hill, looking over the night
As we did together, since forever.

But I will not forget.

The memories may fade, but my love stands strong.

And I lie on the dewy grass, the crescent moon illuminating

Me.

MÓDLMY SIE[1]
Suzanne M.

17 (F) of Missouri, USA

"You have to look into the eyes!"

From below deck where they sat, you could hear the waves slapping the side of the boat. Świętomierz leaned forward, preying on the travel guides' superstition. "If you've found them they'll glow a little - green, maybe blue. Red, if they've been dead for long, but always in the eyes. Elsewhere, they're just dead."

He chuckled at Renard, the youngest guide, whose chin was practically sitting on the ground. Świętomierz wiped his hands on his trousers. They had been sweating ever since they set out, and the perspiration was icy against his palms.

"And they really do leave the ship to find souls to consume?"

Świętomierz looked up. "Eh?"

He had been analyzing the hole in his coat: pushing his fingers through it, seeing how many he could fit in, and wondering if the exploration would be a good one. Finally, he could get the money to buy a new coat. He would buy the one with the double fur lining, even if it meant he couldn't eat for a few weeks. Anything was better than the cold. "Who the hell told you that rubbish? These aren't ghosts--they're alive."

After a few minutes of apprehensive looks among the men, one of them finally spoke up, "Goosefeather told us, sir."

---

[1] *Módlmy się* is Polish for "Let's pray"

"What does that man know? He's just a snobby Englishman." Świętomierz eyed the travel guides with suspicion. "Eh, hey, how much is he paying you?"

"More than enough."

Goosefeather was standing in the entry way of the cabin, looking pissed, frozen, and holding an empty bottle of booze. "And the name is *Goodfetter*!"

He paced over towards Świętomierz, who was trying to look distracted by shuffling a deck of cards, but his fingers were numb from the cold and they kept falling into a scattered mess on the table. Goosefeather slammed the bottle down on the table, almost smashing several of Świętomierz's fingers.

Świętomierz laughed at him. "You must be paying me too little; you aren't so pissed about it."

"I told you to stop drinking, *Why-chore-rick*," he blurted. He was grinding his teeth as usual, upset over his failed attempt to pronounce the impossible surname. Świętomierz thought that perhaps he was trying to grind them away all together so he could live off mashed potatoes.

"It's *vhy-chor-ek*, Świętomierz Wieczorek!" He laughed and banged his fist on the table with an over-dramatic air. He looked to the travel guides and waited for them to start laughing with him, but they never did. "And, I told you if you don't want me drinking, don't give me booze!"

"That wasn't for you!" Goosefeather picked the bottle up, and slammed it on the table again. This time, he didn't miss any fingers.

Świętomierz pulled his hand away and nurtured his swollen fingers between his lips. "Arsehole!"

Goosefeather grinned. "Keep out of my alcohol cupboard. I'm not paying you in booze. And furthermore, you're only on this damn voyage because *you* are the only one who knows what to look for! If you're drunk, how the hell am I going to find anything?"

"You're greedy enough," Świętomierz mocked. "I'm sure you'll find a way."

Goosefeather glared at the drunk with an "I'm better than you" look. He left, and slammed the door behind him as loud as possible.

"You're fearless!" Renard said with wide eyes.

Świętomierz chuckled. "Shouldn't you be on deck telling cranky Goosefeather where to go?"

One of the tour guides, a lanky fellow, spoke up. "He told us to stay with you and make sure you didn't drink."

"All of you? Goosefeather is a loon! Then how the hell is he going to find the ship?"

"We already found it but—" One of the tour guides smashed Renard's toes under his foot. He yelped.

The lanky one spoke again, "We weren't supposed to tell you. Goosefeather said he wanted to look at it himself."

Świętomierz eyed the lanky boy, then looked at Renard. "Renard, I like you more than the others, so tell me: what the hell is wrong with that Goosefeather? Does he think he can just wander around the ship and hope that he doesn't get killed?"

Renard's eyes glowed. "So then it is the right ship!"

"Hell if either of us knows. Goosefeather is either going to be killed or sorely disappointed. Is that why he's smashing my fingers with bottles?" Świętomierz attempted to roll the square bottle across the table.

"Are you going to go save him?"

Świętomierz noticed that the tour guides were looking at him with respect in their eyes. He didn't want to save the jerk, but he liked the idea of having several young natives respecting him. Maybe they'd make him king when they got back to the village.

"Eh, maybe? Would you like if I did that, Renard?" He pulled an unopened bottle of booze from underneath the cupboard and started to pull at the lid.

Renard nodded.

"Well then," Świętomierz finally had the bottle completely open, "*Na zdrowie!*"[2] He put the bottle to his lips and chugged.

Świętomierz crawled haphazardly up the ladder left behind by Goosefeather, with Renard close behind him. He was the only tour guide that dared to come with him. The others were back on the boat crossing themselves and praying. Świętomierz threw himself onto the deck of the boat and hoped not to crash through rotting wood. Renard pulled himself over in the same chaotic manner.

Renard sat up, dusted himself off, and looked over at Świętomierz who was already up and pacing across the ship in search of their lost Englishman.

[2] *Na zdrowie* is a Polish cheer, similar to "Drink up or" or "cheers" in English

"Do you think he's dead?" Renard asked. He looked apprehensive now that he was actually on the "death ship".

"It depends on whether he found them and whether their eyes were glowing." On closer inspection, Renard noticed Świętomierz wasn't looking for Goosefeather, but his bottle of booze.

"Shouldn't we be looking for him?"

Świętomierz took a quick sip from the mouth of the bottle. "Of course, why else would I have come on to this damn ship? I could have gotten drunk on our boat all the same."

Świętomierz casually scoured the deck for Goosefeather while Renard seemed to be searching more seriously at the other end of the ship. Świętomierz toes were starting to feel numb on the ends, tingly. Over the years of dragging them through frozen wastelands, his boots had fallen apart.

Renard found a stairwell leading below deck. "Do you think Goosefeather would have gone down there?" He pointed to the stairs but Świętomierz was too busy drinking from his bottle again to notice.

"He seems stupid enough to wander down stairs like that, dark and creepy. You first." Świętomierz pushed Renard, and he started walking. Świętomierz followed, cautiously looking around and hoping that if something was going to jump out and try to suck the life out of him, he could throw Renard at it instead. Świętomierz tripped over his own foot and they crashed to the floor. He rolled off Renard and moaned.

"Sorry about that."

The dust had jumped into the air. It glowed in the dim light that seeped in through the doorway. The room smelt like the inside of an old book: the scent of dust with a mix of mold, which always reminded him of his grandmother's basement. It had the spider webs to match. Świętomierz stayed close to Renard like he was the one that knew what they were looking for, when really Renard probably knew less than Goosefeather.

They snuck around a corner. Renard screamed and Świętomierz cursed. The body of Goosefeather was curled up on the floor in front of them. It was the human equivalent of a raisin: his skin hung over his bones, wrinkled and dry. He looked paler than before and his mouth was contorted into the shape of what may have been a shriek or a cry to God.

Świętomierz kneeled at the dead man's side.

"What happened to him?" Renard's voice shook.

"They found him."

"I thought you said they don't consume souls!"

"They don't *leave the ship*. They call their victims to them. They've gone for now, they're satisfied." He crossed himself, and folded his hands. "*Módlmy się*. Let us pray that God forgives his soul."

They left the body on the ship. When they returned to the village and civilization, Świętomierz said that Goosefeather had gotten drunk and fallen over the side of the boat at night. His wife didn't need to know the truth.

TO MILGRAM

Calvin R.

20 (M) of Wisconsin, USA

The air was hot, sticky and the horns and steaming stench of Chicago's gridlock filled the bedroom. I pushed away the empty bottles and pizza box with last night's stale crusts.

I was late.

I left the trashy one-room I called an apartment hoping there was sufficient time to walk the six blocks down to their headquarters. My car was in New York with my brother, and in the few short years I had lived in Chicago, I had learned to walk or perhaps summon a taxi to all my nefarious destinations. In my pocket I toyed with a newspaper clipping's furled edges, pulling it out and re-confirming the appointment time, and then stuffing it back into its home. I was pleased to see that it was indeed "8 AM" I had written in the corner with heavy ink. The check, a mere four-hundred and fifty dollars, was forfeit if I were late. However, and they had assured me this on several occasions, if I did decide to show up--and on time--I could keep the money no matter what happened.

The building was red brick, like one of those ancient statues that still stood in the poorest sections of Chicago--certainly no New Haven. I entered into the smallest of lobbies; yellow-lit, cigar smoke trailing through the air and a ceiling fan pumping above my head. An aged black man to my right stared me down as I approached the desk. He was obviously the source of the cigar smoke as a dirty stub lie in an ashtray next to him.

"Mr. Gibbs? Mr. Terrence Gibbs?" the secretary said as she looked down at a manila folder filled with paperwork. Her face was plain, and her blouse stuck to her chest with sweat. She might have been pretty if she had taken the extra effort to make herself up.

"Terry, please. And your name?"

She looked up as if to notice me for the first time. A thin smile appeared on her lips, either happy that someone took the time to notice her or because of my small gesture of informality.

"Anne."

"Nice to meet you, Anne. As promised, I'm here. It's five past, but-- "

"Quite all right, Mr. Gibbs. We've not started yet. Please sign this and then have a seat until we're ready for you."

I signed and walked over to the odd collection of chairs. One was a broken-down recliner and another looked like a high chair. The one I chose was a simple office chair and the cigar smoker sat in a retired hair dryer with its bulbous alien head still attached.

His outfit was about fifty years past its prime: a gray wool suit and suspenders, a rough Panama hat, and a dark wooden cane that he placed his weight on even though he was sitting. He reminded me of when my ex, Jenna, and I worked in the soup kitchens. I saw his type all the time; poor old black men who came in and ate, half-senile and the other half reeking of wisdom just ready to be passed on to their minors. Jenna always took their advice at face value and expected me to go along with it. I never told her the only reason I was there in the first place was that I wanted to get in her pants. Thinking back, she wasn't really worth all that trouble.

I nodded in his direction which elicited only a cold stare. His vacant eyes showed no sign of friendship, and were instead filled with a host of veiny red streaks. I wouldn't dare start a pointless conversation with the man, so I read a magazine lying on the coffee table next to me, some journal about abnormal psychology which was about fifteen years old and falling apart.

The ceiling fan continued to chug. It let out a mechanical hacking, synchronous, and terribly annoying. I crossed my legs and peeked at my wristwatch. As the second hand ticked itself to the top of the watch face, a thirty-something suit came rushing through the door, out of breath. He bent over and grabbed his knees to recover. When he finally rose, Anne was there to hand him a folder, which he promptly opened and put down his signature: J. W----.

"Mr. Gibbs, we're ready for you now," she said as she snatched up a pile of paperwork and stood before the corridor to the back rooms. It looked much too long for such a small building, but I ignored that considering how much space they must have saved on account of the lobby. "Follow me please, gentlemen."

We both filled in behind her. When I looked back at the old man, he did what he had always done--he stared at me with those waxen eyes. Only this time the look was one of suspicion. Or was it contentment I saw?

* * *

She sat us in a brick box of a room with a mirror covering the side wall, and next to that was a door to a separate room. It was much too cliché; as if I couldn't tell there was someone behind it watching my every move.

"Dr. Guile will be here shortly to brief you." Then Anne was gone.

I looked to the curly-haired oaf next to me and it seemed he had the same impression about the mirror. If the unbearable heat hadn't already been a factor, I'd have thought he was sweating just at the sight of it. It was nauseating to think we were going to be participating in some experiment together.

We sat down in the only two chairs in the room; plastic, one was bright orange and the other blue. It was something from elementary school. We were two students sitting in the principal's office waiting for the big man to come in and lay down the law.

My new friend folded his hands and began twiddling his thumbs. An amusing thought came to mind as I watched--he probably had never been sent to the principal's office. Some goody-goody with an office cubicle.

We waited. I wondered what Dr. Guile might be doing that was keeping him. Most likely, he was watching us through that mirror. Maybe that was part of the experiment.

"So what are you going to do with your four-fifty?"

"Excuse me?"

"The money they're giving us. What are you going to do with it?" He smiled, showing a mouthful of annoying toothy gaps.

"Uh... I don't know. Buy a nice stove." I had never really thought about what I was going to spend the money on. Food, rent, booze. Whatever.

"A stove?" he said. "Right...well I suppose whatever the wife needs." He yapped like a small dog.

I gave him my most polite smile and turned my attention to the setup they had in front of the mirror: a big box with a series of switches, a monitor of some sort, a headset, all of which sat upon a metal table protruding from the wall. They were intimidating and confusing; I couldn't quite make out what we might be doing for this so-called experiment. I would just have to wait for Dr. Guile.

The other man shifted uncomfortably in his seat. "Think they're watching us from behind that mirror?"

"How should I know?"

"I dunno. I was just wondering. Hey, let me ask you something."

"What?"

"Do you think they're gonna make us do any sort of puzzles? I had a buddy once who did something a lot like this. He had to put some wooden puzzles together."

"Fascinating."

"It was funny, though, 'cause no matter how hard he tried, he couldn't get his puzzle to work. There were other people in the room too: a couple men, a woman, even a boy. Like twelve years old or something. Well, the men and the woman finished their puzzles and pretty soon it was just my buddy and this boy. He's a smart guy, my buddy, and considering that, he was starting to get pretty mad that all these people got their puzzles together before him. And then the twelve year-old finished his and left. He was so steamed, he ran from the room in a huff. Turns out, his puzzle was never meant to fit quite right. They were experimenting on whether or not he would get all upset. He was, really, even though he said he wasn't that mad. Funny, huh?"

I turned my head away. No matter how much I wanted to punch him in the teeth, I still had to complete the experiment with him. If I was still annoyed afterward, well, I might just follow up on my baser desires.

Dr. Guile entered, not a second too soon, and came over to us in our chairs. It was about time we got this thing started.

"Good morning, gentlemen, thank you for coming. I hope you didn't mind the short wait."

"Of course not," the suit replied.

"Then let's get started." He pulled out two pieces of paper. "In my hand I have two slips. One is marked *Instructor* and the other *Pupil*. Please pick one."

I grabbed one of the slips and opened it: *Instructor*.

* * *

"I'm the Pupil," the suit said. "I guess that makes you the Instructor. So what are you going to teach me, fella?"

Dr. Guile answered for me. "The Instructor's main task is to read off a list of word pairs to the Pupil. During this time, the Pupil will try to remember as many pairs as possible."

"What's all the equipment for?" I asked.

"Good question. Please follow me into this room, gentlemen."

We entered the door that was next to the mirror. There was a chair with two sets of leather straps, which I could only guess were restraints. A metal ledge stuck out from the wall, and on it sat a panel of buttons numbered one to four.

"This is where the Pupil will be located during the experiment," Dr. Guile explained. I was relieved that I was not going to be the one shackled to the chair. "After the Instructor has read the initial list of word pairs, he will begin to name off the first half of the pairs and then will give the Pupil an additional four words to choose from. From the four, the Pupil must discern which word was originally paired with the first half. He will do this by touching either one, two, three, or four here--" the good doctor gestured to the panel, "-- and the answer will be relayed to the Instructor on the other side of the mirror. By the way, neither the Pupil nor the Instructor will be able to see each other. This mirror reflects both ways as you can easily see.

"If the Pupil answers correctly, the Instructor will move onto the next word and keep going in such a fashion until the Pupil answers incorrectly. If the Pupil answers incorrectly, then the Instructor will release an electric charge that will give him a relatively harmless shock."

"Electro-shock therapy?" the Pupil asked. "Is this safe?"

"It's not quite ECT, or electroconvulsive therapy. That is typically done while the subject is anesthetized. We'd prefer to think of this as a slight jolt to discourage the Pupil from choosing incorrectly. The shock is nowhere near lethal. Will the Pupil now please take a seat?"

My friend sat in the chair--reluctantly. "Looks like the electric chair," he said

"I suppose it is in some way," I replied.

With impressive speed, Dr. Guile strapped down his legs and wrists. "Can you reach the panel?"

"Yes, I believe so," he said as he pushed the number one. "I do have a question."

"Go ahead."

"I have a slight heart condition. Nothing major. I was just wondering if the shock would somehow affect that..."

"Not to worry, Mr. W----, the shock is in no way fatal. You'll be perfectly fine."

The doctor and I left him to the other side of the mirror. "It is your responsibility," Guile said, "to make sure the Pupil says the word pairs correctly and to administer the correct voltage should the pairs not match. The machine starts at fifteen volts and thereafter, increases in fifteen volt intervals.

"Now, I'd ask that you take your seat, Mr. Gibbs, so that we might start the experiment."

Guile had pulled over one of the elementary school chairs for me and had taken the other for himself. He handed me a packet of papers stapled together at the corner. The initial page was filled with the word pairs he had mentioned earlier, and I began reading them off into the microphone.

"Lead role, blue bonnet, pretty girl, yellow jacket, jumper cables…" The list was two pages, a lot longer than I could remember in a day, let alone the few minutes it took to read.

"Thank you, Instructor. To make sure everything goes the way it's supposed to, I'll read you the instructions more formally. I ask that you now turn to the third page in the packet. You'll see the first half of each word pair and then a list of four other words, one of which is the second half of the word pair. Please read off the first word and the four options to the Pupil. If he answers correctly, move on to the next word pair. But if he answers incorrectly, you must administer the corrective agent at the proper voltage."

So I read.

"The first word is *lead*. Your options are: one, runner; two, role; three, bomber; four, rank."

I felt myself inhale and hold onto it. A few seconds passed and finally I saw the number two light up on the board overhead. I let go of my breath and read the second pair. This time the wrong number was lit.

"That was an incorrect response, Instructor. Please proceed."

I flipped the first switch labeled *15 Volts*. I could hear the circuit turn on and off, almost feel that power pulse through those wires and into his body.

He got the next word wrong. And the next. Each time I upped the voltage and gave him a shock. The moron wasn't very good at remembering the word pairs, and I was worried that the electricity was only making things worse.

After a little over a dozen pairs, he was up to 180 volts. This time when I flipped the switch, he let out a small grunt. The next wrong pair and switch and he grunted again. I chuckled nervously.

His wrong answers gnawed at me. I willed him to get one correct, just one so he could be spared from the shock for a few moments while he could gather his thoughts. For God's sake, he should at least be getting one-fourth of them right by guessing.

He reached 300 volts. The correct answer was *green apple*.

He pushed button number four. *Grass*.

I shocked him.

"My heart!" I heard him say through the wall. "There's something wrong with my heart! We have to stop the experiment. My heart!"

I looked at Dr. Guile. "Well?"

"Please continue the experiment, Mr. Gibbs."

"Continue? Didn't you hear him? He's having problems with his heart!"

"It is imperative that you continue."

I gave the doctor a good long look. The man next door was having a heart attack and this supposed doctor, a man who swore an oath to help those suffering, merely sat in his chair with a cold look in his eyes. Perhaps he knew something I didn't. Maybe every Pupil tries to stop the shocks with some reason or another. The stupid suit did sign the papers. He was legally obliged to go through with the whole experiment.

I pushed the microphone button and read off the next word pair.

He forced me to send some more volts his way.

"Stop! No! You must stop the experiment. My heart!"

"Doctor," I said. "He needs medical attention."

"Please continue."

"Did you hear me? Did you hear *him*?"

"You must continue the experiment, Mr. Gibbs."

What else could I do?

When he guessed *lawn gnome* instead of *lawn chair*, I was afraid I would hear some terrible wail or maybe a tantrum. I expected more noise, more anger, more bedlam. I wasn't prepared for the bleak and utter silence that enveloped me. The absence of his objections brought me to my worst fears: had he simply grown complacent or was he now hunched down in that chair, lifeless?

"Listen, doc. I'm not going on with the experiment. That man needs help. And fast."

"Please go on."

"I can't."

"The experiment is completely safe, Mr. Gibbs. It is important that you continue. If you stop now, we'll lose all our data."

"Stuff your data, doctor. The man needs you. Or someone at least close to what you pretend to be. I don't want to be responsible for this man's death. You can keep the four hundred dollars."

"Four hundred fifty."

"Whatever. Keep it. I want nothing to do with this little experiment, and if that means forfeiting my money, then fine."

"The money is yours to keep just for showing up, Mr. Gibbs. And you will in no way be responsible for any harm that may come to Mr. W----."

"You guys take all responsibility?"

"Yes, it is in your contract. You cannot be legally held responsible in any way. Now, I must demand that you to return to your seat and continue."

Three more times did I shock that man in the next room. Three more times did I ignore his non-existent cries. I had reached the last switch. The good doctor told me to stop.

"Thank you very much, Mr. Gibbs. We are now at the end of the experiment."

Mr. W---- came out from behind the door and shook my hand.

I nearly fell out of that elementary school chair.

* * *

They explained to me the whole purpose of the experiment.

"My name is Dr. Jonathan Wiles, Mr. Gibbs. I'm a sociologist with the University of Chicago along with Dr. Guile. The whole time you thought you were sending electricity my way, you were really only flipping a switch, nothing more. I never received a single volt. In fact, as soon as the two of you were next door, I removed myself from the restraints.

"The whole thing was an act, Mr. Gibbs. One to fool you into believing you were punishing me. We wanted to see how far someone might go if they were under the supervision of an authority figure. In this case it was Dr. Guile who insisted you continue. You see, Mr. Gibbs, there have been some terrible things in the past that have been done simply because someone has ordered them done. Think of the Holocaust or the slaughtered peoples in Cambodia under Pol Pot. Think of the genocides in Rwanda and Uganda. How could any sort of people do this to one another?

"Most would say they could never go that far. That they could never kill another person even if they were told to. We would very much like to find out if such declamations are true. You were not the first to be tested and go so far, Mr. Gibbs, not the first at all. Don't feel terrible about not stopping, Mr. Gibbs. It's only human nature, Mr. Gibbs."

I slugged Dr. Wiles in the mouth, and shoved Dr. Guile to the floor when he tried to rise. I ran from that room as fast as I could. Anne tried to hand me a clipboard as I went by, but I knocked it from her hands and kept going. The black man was laughing as I went out the door.

Those lousy no-good cheats. They had fooled me, and fooled me good. I didn't even bother with the money, didn't even care any longer. I needed to be gone from there. A million miles away.

And yet as I carried down that sidewalk, I could think nothing else but: *He's alive. Thank God that sonuvabitch is alive.*

TREACLE
Elizabeth C.

15 (F) of North Lincolnshire, UK

Fingers sticky,
Sickly sweet.
Thick and gloopy,
Bad for teeth.

Good on pankcakes,
Puds and more.
Dripping slowly,
To the floor.

Spoon it out,
Onto some pie.
"It's bad for you",
They say; they lie!

It makes me feel,
All warm inside.
You can't eat this,
It's all mine!

Hail Mary
Kelley D.

18 (F) of Texas, USA

She was a beautiful woman, trapped inside of herself. I never knew anyone stronger than my mother, nor more vulnerable. Her strength showed when she stayed up long into the night, mending my clothes, when she worked extra shifts at the hospital so we could buy groceries, when she told my father, "*No, Paul, you can't see her this weekend, you're not allowed.*"

But then came the vulnerability—when she hung up the phone, and cradled her head in her hands. "Hail Mary, full of grace, the Lord is with thee," she whispered. "Blessed art thou among women, and blessed is the fruit of thy womb, Jesus…"

I was nine, and the sound of my mother's whispered prayers was soothing. I left the room to find her rosary beads, and carried them to her almost reverently, opening her hand and placing them on her open palm.

Her fingers twitched, and she opened her eyes and smiled. "Thank you, darling," she murmured, and drew me close to her, stroking my hair—dark, like hers.

"Mama, what did Daddy say?"

She held me more tightly. "Daddy doesn't want you to live with me anymore. But don't worry, angel. I won't let him separate us."

I kissed her cheek and left her to her prayers. Mama was right; no one could tear us apart. It was only natural for a mother and daughter to be together. Mama said so every night when she tucked me in, after I said my prayers.

"Together forever, my sweet girl," she'd say.

"Till Gabriel blows his horn," I'd reply.

* * *

She cried more often as I grew older. Many days I'd come home from school and step from the brisk, autumn air into the dark, stuffy interior of our little apartment, where everything seemed to grow still. Outside, the wind whisked the leaves off the trees, but inside, everything slept—especially Mama.

It was rare for her to be awake when I came home. I didn't mind though. I'd climb into bed with her and begin my homework, timing the scratching of my pencil to her breathing—my own private symphony. When I finished, I'd slip from bed and go into the kitchen, where I would call my best friend. We could only talk for ten minutes. Mama said that Daddy stole too many of our phone-time minutes for me to talk longer.

Mama would wake after dark, when she and I would make ourselves dinner and sit talking until it was time for me to go to sleep. I'd lie awake some nights, when I wasn't tired, and listen to her talk on the phone.

"Don't you dare call your lawyer, Paul. No, I don't want you to send a letter to my attorney. You know I don't have the money for it. No. *No.* You can't talk to her, she's sleeping. Stay away from my daughter, Paul. She's mine. Do you hear me? *Mine.*"

I'd hear the click as she hung up, then the thump as she leaned against the wall, and, sliding her back down the wall, sit on the floor. Some nights I crept from my bed and peeked out my door (Mama always left it ajar). She'd hug her knees to her chest, rest her head on her arms, and cry—soft, miserable sobs that she muffled by covering her mouth or keeping her head down.

"Hail Mary, full of grace, the Lord is with thee. Blessed art thou among women, and blessed is the fruit of thy womb, Jesus. Holy Mary, mother of God, pray for us sinners, now and at the hour of our death. Amen."

I climbed back in bed, and prayed the same prayer. I didn't know what it meant, but Mama prayed it so often that I thought maybe it helped her to feel better. After whispering the words over and over, often in the wrong order, I'd fall asleep, the prayer still falling from my lips.

"Pray for us sinners…now, and at the hour of our death…"

* * *

When I was ten, we spent two weeks studying fairy tales in school. My best friend, Jamie, liked *Cinderella* best.

"It's the most romantic," she said, laying her hand over her heart dramatically.

"It is not," I argued.

"Yes it is. She's stuck in that nasty old cellar, but then her fairy godmother comes and rescues her and she lives happily ever after with the prince. And those mean old stepsisters got what was coming to them."

"And the stepmother," I added.

"Yeah, her too," Jamie said, looking satisfied.

"I like *Beauty and the Beast*."

Jamie shrugged. "That one's okay, I guess, but not as good as *Cinderella*."

"It has a prince too."

"But he's ugly for most of the story."

"I bet he's more handsome than your old *Cinderella* prince," I said. "I bet Cinderella's prince was really mean. She just didn't get to find out since she only saw him that one time before they got married."

"The beast was mean," Jamie pointed out. She looked smug.

"That's because he was sick," I explained.

Daddy was a beast, Mama said sometimes, but it was only because he was sick. Only it was in his head, not in his body.

At first I thought he could go to see a doctor, but Mama told me Daddy didn't think he was sick, so he would always refuse. Then I very cleverly suggested medicines, but Mama said he didn't think he was sick at all, and so didn't do anything to help himself get better.

"He was not *sick*," Jamie protested.

"Was so," I said. "The beast was sick in his mind, and that's why he was so ugly. Once he got better, at the end of the story—that's when he looked good."

"Maybe," Jamie said.

I was glad that Mama kept me away from my father. I had seen only one picture of him. He looked like a beast, with his dark beard and dark, brown eyes. But he was handsome too, which made me think that someday he would get better, and we'd all be together again: handsome Daddy, the beast, exquisite Mama, the beauty, and me—the little rose that kept their love alive.

* * *

I was ten, and the sound of my mother's whispered prayers at night was grating.

I dawdled after school. I didn't want to go home to find my mother either asleep or crying. She said she worked while I was at school or after I had gone to bed at night, but she was always in the apartment at the same time as me, and I didn't know how that could be true.

Maybe Mama had quit, and was going to get a better job.

Jamie and I played on the monkey bars that day.

"Why don't you want to go home?" she asked, flipping upside down. Her pigtails dragged in the dirt.

I shrugged, swinging my legs back and forth, back and forth. "I just don't. I want to stay and play with you."

"My mother's coming to get me in *five* minutes." She held out the number on her hand, spreading her fingers wide.

"How do you know?"

Jamie showed me her new watch from her upside-down position.

"It's pretty," I said, admiring the way its face gleamed in the winter sun.

"Got it for Christmas. What'd you get?"

"Mama made me a new dress, and put some neat patches on my jeans. We had a real big turkey too." Mama hadn't eaten any of it, just told me that it was usually a man's job to carve the turkey, but we could certainly manage. I didn't think we'd done a very good job.

"Cool." Jamie righted herself as a minivan pulled up near the playground. "Do you need a ride?"

I shook my head. "Nope. My mom will come and get me soon." I was lying. We didn't even have a car anymore. Mama said that Daddy had forced her to sell it so that she could fight to keep me.

"Okay, see you Monday!" Jamie waved over her shoulder as she ran to the minivan and settled herself into the front seat.

I trudged home. I had missed the bus, but the walk gave me time to enjoy the fresh air. Besides, it was almost warmer outside on the playground than it was inside our apartment. Mama said that Daddy had been taking her money so we couldn't keep the house too hot.

"But that's okay, isn't it, darling? Hell is a very hot place. Here, in our cool little apartment, we're much closer to God. Your father's house is very warm. You wouldn't like that, would you?"

I shook my head. "No, Mama."

"We're going to be fine," she said. "We're going to be fine." She kissed her rosary beads. "Hail Mary, full of grace, the Lord is with thee…"

I closed the door behind me, and dumped my backpack next to the sagging, old couch. My stomach growled, and I dropped my mittens on the coffee table on my way into the kitchen.

Mama was on the floor, sleeping.

I stopped, frowning, and knelt down beside her. Her crimson rosary beads were wound around her fist, and she was shaking.

"Mama, wake up. Come on, Mama, I'll help you get to your bed."

But when she wouldn't wake, not even when I pried open her eyes, I began to cry, and hurried to the phone. I lifted the receiver before I remembered that I wasn't supposed to use the phone—in case Daddy was listening in—and slammed it back down again. I paced back and forth in front of the telephone, wringing my hands, sniffling, terrified.

There was a bottle of wine open on the counter, but the glass beside it was broken, and its shards lay in a small puddle of burgundy that dripped steadily onto the floor.

Mama said that sometimes when she drank a glass of wine she could think better. Sometimes she drank much more than one glass, and then she'd pull me into her lap—even though I was too big—and tell me that angels were watching over us.

I always thought that maybe she could see herself better when she drank the wine, like the enchanted mirror the beast gave to the beauty. I couldn't remember, though. Did the mirror break in the story? What if Daddy had done this—broken the mirror so that Mama couldn't see clearly?

I called 911, and they took her to the hospital where she worked. They asked me a lot of questions I didn't understand, about what medicines Mama kept in the house and how much wine she liked to drink, and how long it had been since she had let me talk to my father.

They let me stay with her in the hospital, and when we finally returned home, she apologized to me and threw out all the wine in the house. I wanted to ask her about the enchanted mirror, but she fell asleep on the couch nearly an hour before my bedtime.

She had a large bruise on her face, from where she'd struck the ground when she fell asleep in the kitchen, and one of her teeth had been chipped, but she was still my beautiful Mama. Beautiful, beautiful Mama, who'd only tried to use the magic mirror to find a way to break the spell on the beast. Lovely, lovely

Mama, whose eyelashes fluttered in her sleep as she dreamed of ways to lift the enchantment.

Hail Mary, hail Mama, the most beautiful women in the world, fighting to protect their children.

* * *

I was eleven, and the sound of my mother's whispered prayers was frightening.

I was tired all the time now, but I didn't know why. It seemed to suit Mama, though, since I never asked her if I could play at a friend's house, or asked her for help with my homework anymore. After a snack, I would crawl into her bed after school and sleep until I got up the next morning.

When my grades began to suffer, they sent me to a school counselor. I went and sat placidly, but answered very few of her questions.

They sent me to the school nurse, who handed me a cup and instructed me to pee in it. Repulsed, I refused. She assured me that even though this wasn't routine, it would help me to feel more awake. I did as she asked, then, not wanting them to call Mama and upset her by telling her I wouldn't obey (and who knew how much phone-time that would take up?).

They called me back to the office to tell me that my test results had come back positive.

"Positive for what?" I asked.

"For something inside of you that's not supposed to be there. We're going to have to tell your parents about it."

I nodded mutely. This must have been Daddy's doing, though I didn't know how.

Mama agreed when I shared the theory that night, lying in her bed, both of us huddled beneath the old blue comforter.

"I'll take care of you, darling," she said. "Just do what I tell you, and we'll be fine."

I asked if this would make them separate us. "Are you going to get in trouble, Mama?"

"Nonsense. Together forever, right?"

"Till Gabriel blows his horn," I agreed, before drifting off to sleep. It seemed I had done nothing but sleep for the last month, and if I wasn't in bed, I wanted to be. I was always tired, but I didn't know why.

They summoned Mama to appear in court, and to bring me along. I sat on the hard seat with my hands in my lap, wishing I were as pretty as Mama. She looked perfect in the courtroom, wearing a gray suit, high heels, and even a little makeup. She hadn't put any on in months.

I tried to be very still throughout the proceedings, but I was distracted by a man on the opposite side of the room from Mama. He looked like the picture I had of Daddy, but this man didn't have a beard.

Then, when he smiled at me, I knew. It *was* him! Maybe his absent beard meant that he was changing back to the handsome prince, slowly shedding his monstrous qualities along with his facial hair. My heart soared, and I disappeared into a cloud of hope for the rest of the day.

The court went into recess, but there was no playground nearby, so Mama and I just went home.

She took off her shoes and pantyhose, and I followed suit, removing my shiny, buckle shoes and tights. She went into her room; I went into mine. Once inside, I located a sheet of blank paper and some colored pencils, and began to draw the house that Mama, Daddy, and I would all live in once we were a family again. I used a dark brown pencil to sketch an animal pelt in the corner of the drawing, showing that Daddy had left it behind for good. Then I drew rose bushes beneath the windows of the first floor, and felt very accomplished.

I hadn't heard any noise from Mama's room for some time, though, so I left my paper and pencils on the floor and crept next-door, pushing open the door with one finger.

Mama was on her knees in front of her bedside table, where she kept her Bible and rosary. She lit a candle, then pressed her palms together, and prayed,

"Hail Mary, full of grace, the Lord is with thee. Blessed art thou among women, and blessed is the fruit of thy womb, Jesus."

It was getting dark outside, and I don't think I would have seen the gun if the light of the candle hadn't made it glow, lying there on her unmade bed.

I nearly fell over backwards, but somehow managed to make it to the kitchen in silence, where I lifted the phone and called the police. "Hello, police?" I whispered. "I think my mama is going to try and hurt herself. Yes, she has a gun. No, it's a little one. There's only one bullet next to it. It's on her bed. She's praying. No, she doesn't know I'm calling."

I hung up and hurried back to my room, closing the door behind me. There had been a bottle of wine open on the counter.

I sat on my bed, hugging my legs to my chest, like Mama. My heart thudded in my chest, and it was hard to breathe, hard to stay awake, hard to think. *Hail Mary, now and at the hour of our death.*

I heard Mama rise from where she knelt one room over, heard her blow out the candle, heard her bed creak, heard an odd clicking, popping noise. I heard her open her door, heard her footsteps approach. I heard the cars turning onto our street. *Hail Mary, the Lord is with thee.*

Mama was inside my room, sitting on my bed, holding me close. She smelled of roses and wine and smoke, from the candle.

"They're going to separate us if we stay here," she said to me.

"You said they couldn't do that," I said, frightened. She was beautiful—so beautiful—and I felt like I didn't know her at all.

"I know, darling, but it's all right. I have been praying, and God has shown me what to do. Everyone knows a child's place is with her mother, but your father is going to take you from me. He says I'm not taking care of you like I should."

"You take care of me fine, Mama. We take care of each other." My throat constricted. I heard the cars pull up in front of our apartment building, sirens wailing.

She continued like she hadn't heard me. In fact, I don't think she did. "But if I can't take care of you, no one's going to. I'm going to send you someplace safe, where your father can't get to you." *Blessed art thou among women, and blessed is the fruit of thy womb, Jesus.*

Then the gun was in her hand, pointed at my head, and the police broke down the door and it went off with such a bang that I thought I'd never be able to hear anything again. They tell me what really caused all the noise was my screams, but I don't remember doing anything but sitting on my bed, watching my drawing trampled by the policemen's heavy shoes, watching the blood flow from my mother's leg, where she'd shot herself, watching the gun fall from her fingers, and the rosary with it.

Holy Mary, mother of God, pray for us sinners.

A policeman with blue eyes and large ears wrapped me in a blanket as they carried my mother off in an ambulance, followed by a police car. He told me everything was going to be fine, but I was going to live with my father for a while. *Now and at the hour of our death.*

They made photographs in my room, and put things in plastic bags and took them from the house—including the picture I'd drawn of my family: the beast, the beauty, the rose.

And, watching, I realized something. Mama had been wrong, all that time. The beast hadn't been Daddy—it had been something inside of Mama, hiding where not even she could see it, slowly killing her.

Hail Mary, slayer of the beast. *Amen.*

AND THE BRIDE WORE BLACK
Serena A.

14 (F) of Texas, USA

"What a scandal," they'd whisper on the streets. The priest who performed at his funeral, the weeping mother of the unlucky boy, murmurs of the townspeople gathered around the City Square. "Poor, poor girl."

So, was this how it ended? The mother wept, the father remembering, acquaintances patted backs and extended condolences. We're so sorry for your loss, the words seemed to hold some sort of snicker. And the bride said nothing.

Odd, how so many people look so deeply into the end, as if they forgot the beginning. So we look at a life, as ragged and despairing as it may seem, that collapsed- lost all emotion, any feeling, the element of surprise…gone.

* * *

"He loves me," she giggled, holding up her ring finger. "He loves me sooo much." The diamond splendor glittered in the pale moonlight, sparkled in what light the burning lantern offered.

"He sure does," I agreed in monotone. 10 times in a row-and counting.

"Did I tell you? When he proposed, it was like…" she started excitedly, beaming down at the engagement ring.

"You already told me," I said flatly, interrupting her in an energetic retelling of how clean his shirt was, how elegantly the cake was placed in front of her dinner plate, the exact spot where that ring- that ring, that ring- was nestled into leaves of Godiva- "Godiva! Godiva, Becca DuGrey!"- and any other detail that simply required explanation.

She stopped abruptly. "Oh…"

Her voice trailed off. She looked absolutely crestfallen.

The quiet moment was long. I did nothing to stop it. I stood up.

"I have to go now."

She looked up at me. "All right."

There was something about that dead voice, dead tone, dead whatever that tugged at my heart long after I had left. She was so weak, I was supposed to be so strong. To not crumble at every despairing critique- unlike her. To be able to shrug off the twitters, the stares, the pointing- unlike her. I was power. She was not.

So how the hell did Marie get engaged before me? Before me, of all people?

* * *

She had always worn this hideous conch shell necklace, the same vomit-green turtleneck sweater. No makeup whatsoever was dabbed on her blemishes, the unmistakable shame of adolescence. It was worse during lunch, so distracting to carry on a decent conversation with a whitehead-covered countenance, where my eyes strayed to constantly.

No wonder she was so elated when Brendon Parker asked her out.

At first, I didn't think much of it. What was one boy, one geeky boy worth compared to my pile of football players, basketball players, hell, even the track boys- all the males of my choice. It didn't matter who I dated in the end. I dated them all.

Except for one.

Wes was the typical "emo-hottie", one who carried himself with the air of an un-dateable self. Sure, he had the typical future-prostitutes draping themselves over him, but he sort of swatted them away.

I knew. I used to be one of those girls.

I knew the heartbreaking line of, "Let's just be friends."

She would be sitting with me, and I would be minding my own business at lunch. He'd catch my eye, raise one finger for me to come to him…

"Go," she'd say through her mouthful of slimy-looking ham-and-cheese sandwich. "Just go ahead."

And it always happened the same way: me shooting her an apologetic smile, then when I looked back at her from my new spot by him, she wouldn't be there anymore. I'd feel a twinge of guilt in my chest, which would be quickly forgotten in a record of 6 seconds.

"If you had a second chance for anything, what- or who- would you spend it on?" Wes-the-emo-hottie would ask during one of our random 'talks'.

I was itching to say, "You," but, instead I'd answer with something like, "Her," and I'd gesture vaguely to where she had been sitting.

"Her?" he'd repeat. And I'd nod.

So, day after day, lunch always passed like that. My interrogation time.

Soon, the ache of my heart, the illusion that I could have anyone I wanted (shattered), eventually stopped throbbing so wretchedly. It still hurt, but not as much.

Maybe that's why everything came as a surprise when out of the blue, she sprung back into my life and blurted out, "Brendon asked me to marry him."

"You're kidding me," I said faintly, hearing my own voice echo in my ears, my heart stopping. Or pounding.

Whatever it was, it hurt.

"Yeah, we were outside at this coffee shop-" her chatter kept spilling out in breathless spurts, as if she couldn't handle her inhaling-exhaling just yet. "-and I leaned forward and he leaned forward and then I looked down since I heard something clink against my plate, and he stared into my eyes and said, 'Marie'..." she beamed. So proudly, like a mother watching her toddler finally flail and splash across the swimming pool, "...and, well, that's when he asked me to marry him."

I nodded vaguely. I had stopped listening after "Yeah." It was like my mind had just automatically shut down, refused to allow comprehension, that dark bubble of dread welling up from the pits of m blackened heart. I swallowed hard. I should be happy for her. Right?

"Becca? Becca? Beeeehhhhcccaa."

I rose up slowly, gripping the edge of my chair. I couldn't trust myself not to fall. No one would be there to catch me. "I...I have to go now. Umm....I'll tell Mom about you two. She should be happy that her youngest daughter is getting married." And that the oldest isn't.

As I stood up, the last words rushing out of my mouth, adrenaline seemed to trickle into my veins. My legs stood more firmly, my resolve strengthened. I was preparing to run.

"Becca, wait-"

But I was already running. I was flying, fleeing from truth, fleeing from the brutality of a broken, crumpled heart, the stitches torn again- fleeing from reality.

* * *

"I'm so sorry for your loss."

"I wish I could've done something more to help."

"He was a good man."

Sober, grim faces brought the expression "four funerals and a wedding" to life.

Only, there was one funeral.

And no wedding.

"Why did he have to do it?" the was-to-be bride sobbed, burying her face into the shoulder of her would-be destined maid of honor. "Why? He was drunk and he was driving, Becca. Drinking and driving!"

"I'm sorry..." was all I could whisper, biting my lip so hard that the skin broke. Bitter, metallic crimson flooded my mouth. The sting of that tiny ounce of pain was drowned out in the excruciating pain of a loved one lost.

It's odd, isn't it? How "I'm sorry" becomes such a recycled phrase, reiterated so many times it seems to be pressed into your mind, your lips, your soul- becoming an automatic jerk, a reflex...

Small sniffles became tears, and those tears graduated into sobs. The sobs escalated to a long, drawn-out wail. The wretched bride hurled herself onto the lowering, creaking casket, beating the dulled wood with her fists. Thump, thump, thump, the people heard. Thumpthumpthumpthump.

"Why did you have to do this to me, Brendon? Why did you leave me?!"

And then they were edging closer, hands grasping at her dark cloak. But she continued to scream. "You were the only one who ever told me I was beautiful! No one else! Why did you have to..." her voice broke several times, then, like the pathetic last attempts of a bird trying to soar into the sky once and for all, she trailed off, emotions shattered so much that she slowly began to become numb. To her, the world had become just as dead to her as her cold, stone-dead fiancée.

I wanted to stumble forward, pull my best friend from the "aftereffects" of death, whatever that was, to shield her from the pain that she didn't really know.

But, instead, I chose to slip silently out of the crowd, leaving the poor bride in the midst of the agitated parents, the disturbed crowd. "Too close for comfort" didn't matter at the moment.

It was time for her to be strong- on her own.

* * *

The 7 Wonders of the World should be knocked out of our list of "amazings". What should replace it is how realistic, how down-to-earth we are.

We have a title for everything.

What we call "bad" people, the people who disrupt our perfect, unsmoothed character of society are known as "criminals". For the piercing pain we feel in our hearts- "heartbreak". "Love" is the feeling of indescribable joy- even we put a label on something such as that- and, if it is true love, the always-fleeing icon of something that we really can't and don't understand.

So what do you call the average college girl who comes home at 1:00 in the morning to find her younger sister making out with her boyfriend?

I still remember the damp quietness, if you could call it that, as I pitted-and-pattered my way home, as I never strayed from that perfect single-file, imaginary line, as my ears tried to strain out the truly deafening silence broken by an occasional leaf crunching under my feet, or the metallic drops of rainwater dripping from the pipes running down the side of the college buildings. Everything that stayed silent in the early morning becomes so freaking loud.

"Marie? I just came back from the store, do you want chicken or shri-"

I stopped immediately as my eyes laid on a flushed, mussed-hair, shirtless-on-both-counts couple.

What.

I remember my eyes flitting between Brendon, and Marie, then back to Brendon again. My eyes couldn't help but to skim down his shirtless self. Hm. He needed to work out in the gym some more, that complexion wasn't very becoming, and what was with that...that one pack?

And then when my eyes eventually strayed back to Marie, who had the sense to pull on her shirt when I came in. "Marie?" my voice croaked.

Chicken or shrimp instant noodle dinners seemed less appealing at the moment.

I straightened up, let my face harden into a mask of stone-smoothness, allowed my body to form itself into a more formidable being. "Marie, I need to talk to you. Privately."

I looked up in the kitchen, a coffee mug nestled between the palms of my hands as Marie shuffled in like an ashamed puppy.

"What do you think you were doing?"

The words were blurted out. I reached forward, took her chin into my hands, and lifted her face up. "Look up at me. What do you think you were doing?"

Her eyes were still downcast, and remained that way. "I stifheddeenkyouwere-"

"Clearly, Marie. I can't hear you."

She cleared her throat. "I didn't think you were coming home."

I sighed. Yes, of course she answered my question, like a good little Catholic schoolgirl.

"Marie. I'm not joking. What do you think you were doing?"

For a long moment, it was silent. Then she asked, "What do you mean?"

I sighed again, this time was the sigh of an older sister, assuming responsibility.

"Don't you know?" I crossed my arms. "Sooner or later, though I think it'll be sooner than later," I glared at her shortly, "he's going to ditch you. No, he won't remember the kisses that you two shared. No, he won't remember the dinners you've cooked for him, the holding hands, how you loved him and whatever else that you two did. Just drop it, Marie. You're better than him. And getting married in college? You're young, Marie. You're wasting your dreams, your money. Marriage is a crapshoot when you don't have money to put food on the table and pay the bills." I spoke. She listened.

Another moment of silence. Then, slowly, she glared up at me.

"What," she started saying heatedly, "gives you the right to slander my boyfriend like that? Huh? Do you think you can just walk in on us, making out, and call me out like a referee?"

She crossed her arms as well. This was just the beginning.

"For your information, Brendon loves me, and I love him," she said. "Don't you see? He's been the first person to ever love me, to ever say how beautiful I was, and to hug and kiss and hold my hand! What gives you the right to just waltz in and tell me that he's not "good" enough for me?!" She raised her hand for the quote marks.

"Marie, I'm just trying to do what's-"

"Oh, what's best for me? Is that what you're trying to do?" Her eyes widened, she covered her mouth in fake astonishment. "Oh, my, Rebecca DuGrey actually cares about her little sissy for once! Oh. My God."

My mouth was already shaped into a firm line, my voice rose as I fought and clawed and punched back verbally. "Oh, yeah? Well! If you didn't think that I cared about you in the first 19 years of your life, wait till you see me not care! I swear, you're going to go through Hell..."

"You know what, Becca? Guess what?" she pointed a finger at me accusingly. "You can just go to hell. I HATE you. I hate you, hate you, hate you, and I wouldn't care if I saw you burning right in front of my eyes on a stake and never die! You and your precious little "emo-boy" can go to Hell, too!" And she stormed off.

"I hate you" were the words ringing in my ears. Even after she left.

* * *

I met Wes in front of the college library. Ironic, since that was where we first met. I ambled up to him, hands in pockets, the perfect picture- of devastated innocence.

"You're supposed to be at the funeral, aren't you?"

It was something everyone in the school knew, one of those stories that couldn't help but to tell itself. I flinched at the point-blank frankness. Now, the guilt was starting to seep through the edges of my heart- like a poison, like an unenviable disease, something contagious.

"It was...it was too much." I wasn't lying; it really was. "I just couldn't handle it."

Shrugging, he looked off to the side, nodding somewhat agreeably. "I," he replied quietly, "know how you feel."

Of course he did. That is, he knew how I felt, since he didn't even attend Brendon Layne Parker's- his own brother- funeral. God. How we torture ourselves, how we can inflict so much pain in our lives- more than 'thine own enemies'. We are our own worst critics.

Everything became silent

Was this the time for impulses? To drop all guards, lower the insecurity, to silence the doubting voice inside me?

"Wes," I said. "Wes, ask me that question about second chances. Ask me that again."

"Becca-" he started. I cut him off.

"Just say it." My voice was strained, everything was starting to fall apart. Sooner or later, I'd lose control and…and crash.

Wes sighed. "Okay…" Pausing, as if he was thinking back to that day when he first asked me that same question, he finally said, "Becca, if you could have a second chance for anything, what-"

Everything happened so fast, in that split second, from when I said, "You," to when I turned towards him, in that moment as I leaned up and kissed him- everything seemed to happen when he tensed, then relaxed and finally, for once, let his guards down, his arms wrapping around my waist to when he kissed me back.

Finally. "You."

* * *

You thought that everything would end perfectly, didn't you?

You thought that I, Becca DuGrey, would end up "all right", my heart stitched back together ("This time, the stitches should hold, ma'am"), that we can end this story with a "happily ever after", right?

Well, you're right.

I did end up happily every after, for the most part.

But the bride, my own sister, didn't.

* * *

"We are here today, gathered in the presence of.."

A drop ran down the side of her face. She stirred.

"-these two beloved, Wesley Peter Parker, and Becca Madeline DuGrey…"

Everything felt so wet. So liquidated, no stronghold.

"Do you, Wesley Peter Parker, so swear to keep her in sickness and in health, to honor this sacred union, and…"

A frail hand feebly reached for that cold, hard stone. One finger brushed against the indented tablet, taking a small layer of dirt and dust with it.

"I do."

The other hand groped for sharpness, the taker-of-life, yearned for the coldness and brutality. She forcibly carved the blade deeper into her flesh, gritting her teeth in denial of any physical pain. The drops turned into crimson streams of blood.

"And do you, Rebecca Madeline DuGrey, take Wesley Peter Parker for your husband, and swear to care for him, in sickness and in health, to honor this sacred union…"

Only a few more minutes now. Only a few more minutes until she was out of this pain, out of this heartbreak, out of the weak shell that, fittingly, housed such a weak spirit. It only took a death for her to break down into pathetic pieces.

She closed her eyes peacefully. She could feel the life slowly slithering out of her, to finally bring her to a better place. Where he was.

And with another stab, another thrust, another blossom of pain, the life fled from Marie Klein DuGrey.

"I do."

SYLVIA
Kelly A.

20 (F) of California, USA
If you look through the dipping boughs
of the elm trees
you can see the glittering patches
of light -

that is her genius.

hidden beneath shadow layers of
cotton and year
are the shards that splinter
like little foot bones
and tear at rational thought.

to brave the new world
would be a wondrous thing,

it's all just a beautiful
dream.

two by two they fall
the haunting obituary of silence.

THE OIL FIELDS ARE BURNING
Kylan R.

15 (M) of Oregon, USA

NEW YORK CITY, NEW YORK

"The question is," Director Mark Clevenger said, pacing at the head of the conference table, tie loosened and sleeves rolled up passed thick forearms, "Is when to strike. Obviously the public isn't ready for this yet. It will never be ready. If we hopped onto the market band-wagon today, right now, we'd be crushed. It doesn't matter that our technology is superior. The IU would do what they've been doing for twenty years. " Clevenger bent forward and pounded his fist on the table, "Destroy the opposition over night."

The twenty-seven board members and majority shareholders of SoftFuel sitting around the mahogany conference table were silent. Impassive. The director was right. He was always right. Mark Clevenger – a Napoleon of corporate tacticians – commanded an unspoken respect from his shareholders. Business was a game of chess for him. He made his moves with the entire game board in view and piece positions already analyzed. Clevenger knew what he was talking about. The director didn't need yes-men and he didn't need no-men. He needed a sounding board. That's why they were there: to help his ideas resonate.

Clevenger eased into his chair and quietly poured a cup of coffee. *Screw the doctor. Screw decaf,* he thought to himself as he drank deeply from the mug. *And screw my heart palpitations.* Caffeine would be necessary today. Making plans for a war was tiring stuff. Clevenger knew.

He set the mug down and massaged his temples. "Something has to be done. If we ever want our fuel cells available to the world, something needs to be done. And none of this 'government sponsorship' crap. We need to take matters into our own hands. You know how much money we've got collecting dust and interest in the bank right now? One point six billion. We can do practically anything with that much money." He took another sip of coffee, "But even with all that cash we still can't stop the Iranian Unity from crushing us. No one can. People broke apart OPEC only to have Iran go all expansionist and take over every middle eastern country with major oil fields within it's border in the Oil Wars. Now the middle east *is* the Iranian Unity. Therefore they own over half of the world's oil. We all thought OPEC was bad. This is much worse. They control the oil market. They have a bona fide monopoly going on. Anytime a new fuel source or oil retrieval technique comes into play, the IU lowers their prices dirt cheap so that no one wants to buy the more expensive energy source. Eventually, the alternative fuel company will go out of business and then the oil prices shoot right back up without the competition. *Classic.* This will happen to us when we market our fuel cells. Why wouldn't it?"

Clevenger rose back to his feet – mug in hand – and made his way to the wall window over looking the chaotic streets of New York. He watched his reflection in the glass over the steam from his coffee. "Can anyone tell me what they would do in a situation like this?" Silence. Of course not. *He* was the one who sat at the head of a table. *He* was the one who ran a company. *He* was the multimillionaire. How should they know?

"No takers?" The board members squirmed. "Well, I know what I would do," Clevenger turned around and drained his mug, "Fight. Fight for supremacy. Destroy the IU."

Marty Mather, a majority shareholder of his, suddenly snorted, "Is that coffee Irish? Get a hold of yourself, Mark. The IU's a *country*. We are a *company*. How would we fight the richest country in the world? We have no military. We have no ambassadors. Nothing." Murmurs of agreement passed around the table.

Clevenger smiled. "Money can buy any gun,"

"I'm really hoping you meant that figuratively, Mark," Mather said.

Clevenger's smile only broadened.

"You mean you want us to *attack* the IU. With guns and bombs?" Tim Brody, another shareholder said incredulously, "I thought I'd never say this, but you're insane."

"In the battle of Thermopylae, three hundred Spartan soldiers killed twenty thousand Persian invaders-"

"I don't want a history lecture, Mark. This is different."

"Not really."

"Really." Mather returned, "Besides, every Spartan at Thermopylae was slaughtered. So they killed a couple thousands of Persians before they died - "

"Even if we 'died', Marty, the world would be a better place. No more monopoly. Fair fuel prices."

Marty rolled his eyes, "Don't give me this 'for the good of mankind' crap. You're not a hero, Mark. None of us are. We're survivors. We're exploiters. We're *businessmen*. We steal from the poor and kill babies. It's what we do."

Clevenger turned back towards the window and watched the flood of taxis circle around SoftFuel's base. He knew what was best for the company. This fight for survival would be the takeover of a lifetime. It didn't matter what the board members said. It was by his sweat, his blood, his back that SoftFuel was formed. He wasn't crazy. He was a visionary. *Corporate war.* He smiled at the thought. There was a first time for anything. SoftFuel would survive.

Like a father, Clevenger knew what was right for his baby.

"Do any of you know what the fuel market is worth right now? Do you know how much money the UAE brings in every year. There's a reason why they are the richest country in the world, boys. Oil really is black gold." He paused, letting the question sink in.

"Seven trillion dollars. Seven thousand billion. Every year."

The sounding board was silent.

"Do you realize that if our fuel cells got a fair chance in the world market, the flow would be re-directed from the IU's treasury and *we* would be the ones earning that nest egg?" He shook his head. The shareholders held their breath behind him. Seven trillion. A lot of money. Each of them silently wondered what he or she would do with a slice of such a sum. A company of their own. An island. A yacht. No, make that three. Whatever Clevenger had in mind suddenly didn't seem so crazy. He was right.

As always.

"But how would we do it?" Marty asked, shaking his head, "Thermopylae is one thing. The Iranian Unity is quite another."

"Not really."

"Enlighten us, boss. What could you possibly have in mind?"

Mark Clevenger returned to his seat at the head of the table. "What is said at this table, stays at this table. There is no talking about this to spouses. Not to reporters. Not to your kids. Not to your *dog*. If there is anyone who doesn't think he can follow through with what I *order* from this point on should leave now and had might as well sell his shares. Because he is not on this board anymore." Clevenger eyed the group, waiting. Waiting for the weak to leave. Tim Brody sighed and stood.

"You're crazy, Mark. This is crazy. I don't know what you think you're doing." He fingered his briefcase for a moment, eyebrows arched, looking at the director in disbelief. He shrugged and headed for the door. "I'm out." Chairs scraped across the granite tiling and two other men followed Tim. Four more left the table. Another three. Only seventeen board members left.

Clevenger stared at them expectantly. "Anyone else?"

Silence.

No one else.

"Good," He said shortly, "You are the lucky ones. I'm about to tell you how a seventeen men can break down the richest country on the planet and earn several trillion dollars while they're at it." Clevenger poured another cup of coffee, smirking at the smell. Good, caffeinated stuff. He would need it.

"Like I said," he grinned, sipping his coffee, "The question is when to strike."

TENANCINGO, MEXICO

In a swift erratic jump, the red-tailed hawk caught the vole; wings outstretched, eyes gleaming. Fresh meat. The small animal wriggled in the hawk's talon, squealing. It's small furry body was arched in pain, head twisting, limbs flapping like some obscene rag doll's. *Save me,* it seemed to scream. To this the hawk replied, *No hope, no hope.* Tightening it's claws as the bird prepared to fly, the red-tail shattered the vole's skeleton in it's vice grip.

And emotionless, the hawk shrieked and took flight.

Ali Kemal watched the hunt with a smile, sitting on a small bench outside of the dusty Catholic church, overlooking a near-empty street way with several cars and bicycles parked along the side. All dusty. Everything was dusty here. Everything was washed-out. Like an old western movie. Dull colors, bad actors. Normally, these dusty western roads would have been filled with sweaty boys playing soccer, or sweaty men playing cards, or sweaty women buying food. But it was empty this morning during mass. Everyone was sitting in the church behind him. Undoubtedly, soiling the pews.

So Ali closed his eyes and replayed the hunt. It had been beautiful. Exquisite: the way the little animal had arched it's spine in death. The pain that had resonated from the vole was like a high to him. Nature's cocaine. The blood that had welled up beneath the talons, the bones that had broken, the frantic screams. The whole package. For Ali, there was something irresistible about another person's pain. Intriguing and mysterious. But beautiful. Always beautiful. Death was like a dance, but there was no pattern, no specific moves. It was impromptu. Like a painting, like a poem. Ali shuddered as he imagined the vole in his clutch, squeezing it slowly, so that the life and the pain oozed out. It felt good. He felt ten feet tall. Turned on by the silent screams.

I am the hawk.

And for that reason, I am trapped in this sleepy Mexican town, surrounded by oblivious farmers, staying my hand, waiting. Ali Kemal was always waiting. Waiting for a job. Waiting to exercise his talents. His passion. Each and every day, he waited to play the part of the grim reaper again. And waltz to the seductive dance of dying. In this town, for these people, Ali put on a mask. The mask of a rich but quiet Turkish eccentric. They didn't know his real face was a skull.

I am the hawk.

Footsteps thudded on the veranda planking as a man came up beside him and leaned against the church wall. Ali did not look up at him. There was silence for several moments as the both of them stared out into the road.

And then the man asked, shoving a box of camels at Ali, "Cigarette?"

Quietly, Ali accepted a cigarette, pulled a lighter from his own pocket and lit up. Without a word. Without looking at the man's face.

Some more silence.

"Did you hear the Cubs and the Yanks played last Saturday?" The man finally asked.

"Really? What was the score?"

"It was a tie."

Ali smiled to himself and pulled on the cigarette. A job. Finally. "You may sit down, Mr. Clevenger. It's been a long time."

"Ten years, I think" Mark Clevenger said, taking a seat on the bench. He glanced around the street and church. "Nice place you chose. Quiet. Obscure. Hard to find. Had to go through seven people to get to you."

Ali frowned, "Seven? That's all?"

"It's enough. Trust me."

"Tell that to Interpol."

Clevenger shrugged and tapped out a cigarette of his own. "I have a job for you, Kemal."

"Ah, like the good old days."

"Not like the good old days. This project will be the biggest, highest paying you will have ever taken on."

Kemal smiled. A challenge. "Try me, Mr. Clevenger."

Mark told him his plan. As he ended, a choir began to sing in the church behind them. The faint Spanish found it's way out the open double doors as Kemal brooded in silence. What Clevenger had in mind *was* crazy. The ten SoftFuel board members may have been right to walk out.

But I am the hawk.

"Will it work?"

"That, my friend, is up to you. If you choose to accept, that is."

"*How* will it work? The politics of all this is beyond me."

Clevenger took a drag on his cigarette and tapped the ashes off with a flick. "When the IU invaded three quarters of the Middle East in the Oil Wars, it was solely for profit. They recognized the massive income that forty or so oil fields could generate. They recognized they could become a world power overnight. They wanted to expand. The IU also had the guts and the means to pull it off. Iraq fell, Kuwait fell, Oman fell, Saudi Arabia, Qatar, Egypt. Anywhere that there was a drop of oil, they took. But that left numerous smaller unconquered countries scattered all around their borders: Israel, Jordan, Lebanon, the UAE, Yemen, Armenia -"

"Old news, Mr. Clevenger. Get to the point."

"Patience, my friend. You of all people should know that."

"You sound like my mother."

"The same one that dumped you in the streets at five? Words of wisdom, alright."

Ali only smiled.

"Anyway. It was only until recently that the IU decided they wanted a united Islam. A united Caliphate. One whole middle east. That means more expansion. They have called on the unconquered countries to hold a referendum in order to join their Unity." Mark grinned and blew out a cloud of smoke. "But who would want to join those oil whores? Half of the unconquered countries refused to hold a referendum, and the other half had their citizens vote, but the proposal failed anyway. The IU is a dictatorship. The other countries saw as much. But now the IU is angry and is prepared to take these countries by force. Tempers are flaring. The atmosphere is tense. There's already been a bombing outside of an IU embassy in Armenia. The middle east is ripe for another war."

The church-goers stopped singing. Ali flicked his camel into the street and sat back.

Clevenger continued, "To make matters worse, there's a man – Mustafa Sabradan: charismatic, rich, a wonderful speaker – who's come out of the woodwork and is vigilantly preaching against the IU. He claims they're as bad as America, that they've adopted consumerism as their God. He's pretty much painting the IU as the devil himself. And he's wildly popular; practically all of Islam agrees with him. Thousands of people attend his public speakings. The Muslim public wants *him* as a Caliph to rule the middle east, not some power hungry oil sheik from the IU." Mark stared at a wooden carving of the Virgin Mary above the church doors, hands crossed in front of her breast, face serene. "And that, Kemal, is where you come in. By assassinating Sabradan, the non-Unity Muslims will automatically assume that it was the IU who killed their precious leader. They will strike back. Sabradan operated out of Amman, Jordan and he and his members hold open conferences every Thursday evening. As soon as Sabradan is killed his followers will convene and discuss...the turn of events. You will be there that night and suggest that bombing the IU's oil processing plant is the most impacting option."

"Starting a war. That *is* new."

"A necessary war."

Ali frowned. "It all seems so unreliable. So risky. It would be very easy for the project to fail."

"Either way, you get a sizable pay check." Clevenger paused, "Will you take the job?"

Ali Kemal glanced around the veranda and street. The sleepy Mexican town of Tenancingo. How he would miss it. "Of course. Expect Sabradan to be in the headlines by the weekend. And by Monday morning the oil fields will be burning."

Clevenger nodded and stood, straightening his jacket, "How can I contact you?"

"You can't." Ali winked. "Too many bugs in the system. *I'll* contact *you.*"

The church bells rang – loud and reverberating – and a reedy organ started up inside the church. Like water behind a broken dam, the church-goers immediately began filing out - dusty, as always - and ignored the American stranger and the Turkish eccentric on the bench beside them.

Mark shrugged and nodded again at Ali Kemal. "Good luck." And without another word he promptly spun on his heel and disappeared around the side of the church.

Ali stared off into space, frowning to himself. Had he really just agreed to take that job? The project was madness: anyone in his line of work would have known that. Clevenger was foolish to the point of being insane. One man, one company could not start a war. Ali stood and made his way home to pack. But he was not so sure anymore. Clevenger had so much ambition. *And* his "perfect storm" scenario seemed as if it could possibly work. Besides, Ali thought, this was a chance to slake his thirst. To waltz the dance of death. To create beauty in ending a life. And it *was* beautiful. Always beautiful.

Ali was nodding now. Yes, this could work. He would make this work. Clevenger had been right to choose Ali Kemal for his war-starting. He was right to choose Kemal in altering history. To choose him to kill and enjoy the killing.

Because I am no ordinary assassin.

I am the hawk.

DAMASCUS, SYRIA

The crosshairs were centered on his face. The same face which was plastered on billboards and printed on propaganda pamphlets all across the non-Unity middle east. It was chiseled, hard, and persuasive. The face of a politician. As he squinted through the scope, Ali Kemal wondered how Sabradan's features would look as it contorted in pain, a bullet in his chest. Shocked, definitely. But perhaps also angry, resigned, hopeless. It would be a treat to find out.

The high riser Kemal had posted himself on was to the far left of the parliament square. Out of the way, out of sight, and out of mind. An ideal sniping location. From the gritty, feces stained ledge Kemal had a clear shot to Sabradan's podium. The podium behind which he would make his final speech. He smiled as he watched the self-made politician rise from his seat and make his way toward the microphone. The gathering crowd roared. They screamed. They chanted his name.

Sabradan was a god.

A god in a pinstripe suit and horn-rimmed glasses.

Speak to us, the people cried. *Enlighten us. Throw more mud at the IU.* The underdog now had a powerful inspiration. And suddenly they weren't feeling so small anymore. Ali knew if this man asked these people to go to war with him, they would drop their children, their jobs, their bill payments and rush for a gun. Yes, they would all be slaughtered. Each person in the crowd knew that. But they didn't care. Sabradan could command them by simply turning on charm. Kemal was fascinated.

The man shuffled a stack of paper at the podium and scanned the crowd before him. He smiled, "Citizens of Armenia, Jordan, Lebanon, Syria, and the UAE! And citizens more importantly of Islam! Of Allah!" He paused and spread his arms wide, "I salute you!"

A roar. Stomping feet. Clapping hands. Ali Kemal flipped off the safety of his gun and slipped his finger into the trigger guard.

Mustafa Sabradan held up his hands. *Calm down now, children.* "I stand here, this afternoon, a humble servant of the free public, of God, of the world. I stand here before you, your servant!"

Another roar.

"My friends! It has come to my attention that the government and the public of Afghanistan are seriously considering holding a second Iranian Unity referendum. A recount of sorts. They are unsure. They are doubtful of our influence in this matter of a second middle eastern war. Afghanistan does not want bloodshed. They do not want their young men – sons and husbands – traipsing off to another senseless war." Sabradan paused again. He sighed audibly and swept off his glasses, "But I must warn you, Father Afghanistan, that joining the IU will strip you of your freedom, of your religion, and of your family. No war is senseless when fighting for these things. I call on you Afghanistan. Never give in. Never stop fighting. The children of your sons and young men will praise their fathers' names, as they praise Allah, if they fight today for a better future for the countries of the middle east! My friends, my brothers and sisters, my fellowmen! We are in this together! Don't you see? We must unite against the Middle Eastern manifestation of America and defeat – whether with swords or words – the Iranian Unity!"

The politician punched the air and the crowd went wild.

"Sabradan, Sabradan, Sabradan!"

Screaming, they waved the flags of non-Unity countries in the air, fluttering in the smoggy, polluted wind. They surged towards the podium, fully overcome with patriotism and anger and pride, reaching for his hand. A touch, that was all they needed. A brush from the hand of their god dressed in a pinstripe suit. Tears streamed down Sabradan's face as he punched the air again. This did not go unnoticed by the crowd. He was a good actor, Kemal thought. Manipulating emotions by being emotional. So unfortunate such promising talent would have to be terminated. Kemal breathed deeply as he stared at Mustafa Sabradan through the scope. One shot: the end.

Now.

Kemal pulled the trigger. Below, standing at the podium, surrounded by adoring followers, Sabradan jerked back, half of his skull blown away. Bits of bone and flesh splattered the foreign dignitaries sitting behind him. His mouth open in a silent scream, Sabradan took one step forward and fell. He feel into the hands of the onlookers. An obscene crowd surfer. Several people caught him, shocked. Silence fell like a blanket of snow. And slowly, gradually, screams returned. This time angry, horrified.

Ali Kemal closed his eyes and let the entire scene wash over him. Beautiful. Always beautiful. He soaked in Sabradan's pain, his dying breath, the blood on the podium. He was the grim reaper ferrying souls from this world into the next. He was the hawk. Kemal inclined his head slightly towards the dead man below as he proceeded to dismantle his gun. *Thank you for the dance.*

Latching his gun case, Ali Kemal stood and headed for the rooftop door, listening to the cries of the people gathered in the parliament square, *"No hope, no hope."*

AMMAN, JORDAN

The mob filled the meetinghouse. There was no room to walk or sit, let alone breath. The people merely stood and shouted in outrage. Argued, swore, prayed, threatened. Sabradan was dead! Blood needed to be spilled. Preferably the IU's. It was no secret that the middle eastern superpower had assassinated their leader. It did not take a genius to work out whose gun had blown a hole the size of a golf ball in Sabradan's head. Obviously, they had been feeling threatened. Mustafa commanded too much power. He was unsafe. Potentially dangerous. And the big dogs wanted to play alone by any means necessary.

Ali Kemal elbowed his way through the swarm, his face bowed, towards the head of the room where Sabradan's staff sat. *So angry,* he thought. How could one man be the cause of such emotion. The tears. The sobs. The yells. A great man in life, an even greater man in death. Kemal smiled to himself as he pushed his way to the front of the crowd. Funny how such things worked.

He stopped at the front and waited patiently as one of Sabradan's eight cabinet members rose to their feet and walked up to a microphone. The man was tired. Harassed. Hopeless. His tie was loose, his eyes looked dark and sunken. Sighing, the man held up his hand for silence, "You're attention, please."

The people quieted immediately. The man rubbed his eyes. He paused for a long time, staring nowhere in particular. Finally he whispered, "We have been dealt a devastating blow. Mustafa Sabradan was a great man. A true visionary. A fearless leader. He knew what was right for us all and he was willing to take a stand for it. A stand that got him killed. He...he was murdered for *us*. For you. For me." The man trailed off and stared into the faces of the crowd. Kemal smirked. Sabradan was suddenly a Christ for the Muslims. An atoning sacrifice. What did that make him? The man who had nailed this political Jesus to a cross? Inwardly, Ali shrugged.

Close enough.

The man shook his head, "But this isn't his funeral. This isn't a eulogy. I'm not going to waste my time speaking well about the dead. You know, I know, *we* know something has to be done. Mustafa Sabradan will not go unavenged. By killing our leader, the IU has started a war. A war which won't be ended overnight. They started a fire. One that won't be stamped out easily. What did Sabradan teach us? That we are indomitable. There is no force on earth that can make us submit unwillingly with mere bombs and guns. Our pride will live on."

Ali decided to speak up, "How will we fight? We have no army. No air force, navy. No funds."

The crowd murmured.

The man shrugged. "We have numbers. We have will power. There is not —"

"How well do you think your 'will power' will stand up against a machine gun?" Ali cut in.

The man stared at Ali for a moment. "Who are you?"

"I'm saving your ass."

The crowd murmured again. It was appalling how disrespectful this young man was. The old *kids these days* expression was undoubtedly being tossed around the room, whispered disapprovingly. Ali could almost hear it.

"So you are saying that our freedom is a lost cause? Are you implying that the IU has already won?" The man said quietly, "Because if these are your sentiments I suggest you find the door. This is neither the time nor place for an argument."

Ali smiled. "Of course not. I love my country as much as the next man. The IU is cultural suicide. I know that. You know that. I'm just saying launching a war against *the* richest country in the world is unwise. Especially when we have no coherent plan."

"But that is the purpose of this meeting. *Planning.*"

"I can help you."

"You have no military rank. Maybe a little experience in war, at best."

"You don't know that. And besides, is that how we define a person. Social standing?"

"Generally, yes."

"I can help you," Ali repeated.

The man sighed and looked out into the crowd. And then, wordlessly, he stepped aside and gestured at the microphone. *All yours.* Ali Kemal grinned to himself and stepped up onto the platform. Frowns and hard stares met him as he looked at the faces of the mob. He could already tell they would be an open-minded audience.

He told them Clevenger's plan.

Silence.

Finally, a man in the audience raised his hand, "You want us to bomb the Central Oil Processing plant? But half of the world's oil supply is refined there."

"Without oil, there is no IU. That simple. Besides, with such a steep drop in oil production other fuel forms will be able to flourish from out of the shadow of a fuel monopoly." Ali returned.

"There comes a point where being bold is just being stupid."

"They'll never see it coming."

"We are not terrorists."

"Of course not. The IU, however, is." Ali said with a smile, "Like I said, since the IU stores *all* of their oil in one central location, knocking them out would be incredibly easy. One blow. Alluding to the Christian bible, David slew the giant with a single stone."

The silence was defeaning.

A man stepped forward, flanked on either side by an armed body guard, pushing through the wall of bodies Ali immediately recognized him as the Prime Minister of the UAE. He squinted up at Kemal.

"Sabradan was a wise man and a good friend. I can't imagine him not supporting this venture," He looked down at his feet, "I can provide one hundred men, weapons needed, and any aircraft necessary. I will need another hundred volunteers, though. You can find me at the embassy until morning."

He then turned on his heel and pushed his way back towards the door.

Ali turned back to the speechless crowd. He smiled.

"And now I'll ask. Who's with me?"

OUTSKIRTS OF RIYADH, SAUDI ARABIA

"Drone now in a holding pattern. We can pickle the target at any time, sir. I'm counting that the target has five or six SAMs, though. So these guys aren't taking any chances."

Behind the sand dune, lying on his stomach, Captain Wazir El Sayad slowly lifted the radio to his mouth. He sighed, "Continue holding pattern. I don't want you anywhere near that plant. If they get one lock on you, you are *mort*, to use an French euphemism. Stone cold dead."

"Yessir. I understand, sir. Over and out."

El Sayad lowered the radio and squinted over the dune rise at the sprawling plant nestled in the hills below. It was a formidable target. The prime minister was gambling. Gambling everything. His country, his job, his *life*. If the mission failed, the IU would declare war on the UAE immediately. No questions asked. What he ordered in the field tonight would determine the outcome of the lives of millions. After tonight, the world would never be the same, one way or another.

And someone would be waking up with a splitting headache.

El Sayad shook his head. Three days ago he had been in Paris. *Paris*. The city of love. The city of fine wine and even finer women. The city where no one remembered the night before. Absolute heaven. And he had been dragged out of that paradise to make war with the most powerful country on earth. Instead of the Eiffel tower on the skyline, he was seeing fifty foot oil distillation columns. Instead of holding the stem of a wine glass, he was holding a gun. He had to seriously reconsider his lifestyle.

What am I doing here?

What are *we* doing here?

Five hundred miles away in a military bunker, he and his men and ninety-something volunteers had been briefed about the mission. His superiors had said that by destroying the IU, what he and his men did tonight would not only liberate the Middle East, but free the *world* from the IU's unstoppable fuel monopoly. By destroying the IU's entire supply of oil, – half of earth's fuel – they would destroy the Unity itself. In fact, they had practically described oil as the devil's piss. That black gold came from lakes of fiery brimstone. Destroying it would be ridding the world of a terrible addiction. And yet, when El Sayad thought of the billions of cars and jets and boats oil powered he felt doubtful. He felt like a petty terrorist. What he was about to do today didn't feel like heroism, it felt like they were tearing down another pair of world trade centers. It just seemed wrong. Where was the logic? Burning the oil was like burning money. Who would do such a thing?

What am I doing here?

Beside him, in the sand, a small pager beeped and a single word scrolled across the LCD screen, glowing redly.

Execute. Execute. Execute.

The magic word had come: it was time. Frowning, El Sayad lifted the radio to his mouth again, eying the pager, "Ground to bird. Ground to bird. Deliver the package. I repeat, bomb those crude oil whores back to where they belong. Out."

"Roger, sir. It will be a pleasure. I'll see you back home."

El Sayad grunted to himself and nodded to his second, who quietly spread the word among the prostrate soldiers. Whether he liked it or not, the good captain had just signed a death warrant.

Execute.

Heads would roll, indeed.

* * *

Ali Kemal crouched nearby, - out of sight, out of mind - staring at the two hundred soldiers lying fifty feet away, waiting for the orders to invade the COP plant. According to Clevenger's instructions, he wasn't supposed to be there. He was supposed to be miles away in some motel room, waiting. Waiting for news. Waiting for payment. Well, Clevenger wasn't God. He wasn't Santa Claus. Ali didn't need to be good, for goodness sake. What Clevenger didn't know, wouldn't hurt him.

Ali smirked. For now, anyway.

The radio at his feet crackled to life, "Ground to bird. Ground to bird. Deliver the package. I repeat, bomb those crude oil whores back to where they belong. Out.

"Roger, sir. It will be a pleasure. I'll see you back home."

Ali smiled. It was time. He held up a hand and gestured towards the soldiers. Behind him, twenty five special ops crept over a dune rise. Each carried a high caliber machine gun and four hundred rounds. Ali Kemal expected them to paint the sand red that night. He expected the discharging bullets to make beautiful music. And he would dance to it. Waltz, actually.

Because he was the hawk.

* * *

The drone screamed over head like some nocturnal bird of prey, engines glowing orange and heated exhaust rippling the air behind it. El Sayad watched it carve it's way towards the plant, pregnant with a thousand pounds of explosives and motioned for his men to move. Silently, they climbed over the dune, specks in the night, and began jogging for the plant.

Execute.

A powerful word. El Sayad's heart thumped inside it's cage, bruising his ribs. He was being a terrorist! He was sure of it. The entire mission felt wrong. Underhanded. Poorly thought out. That drone would plunge the world into chaos. Chaos that would result in war, in poverty, in destruction. It would do more than put a stake through the heart of the IU, it would put a take through the heart of the world.

But El Sayad shook his head, bit his lip, and kept jogging. Orders were orders.

The drone was less than three hundred yards now from the plant and eating the distance fast. El Sayad watched it, mouth set, face grim. *May Allah save my soul. This is madness.*

His radio crackled. "They've got me locked, sir. That was way too quick. I don't have much time before they send up a couple of Surface to Air Missiles."

El Sayad's heart fell. "What!?"

"They're launching one! It's locked onto my engine." The pilot swore, "Deploying hot waffle."

Sure enough, a trail of smoke hissed from behind the walls of the plant, heading immediately for the drone. Several of his men stopped mid step to watch.

"*Najis*," El Sayad swore.

Two glowing heat charges were ejected from the drone and into the air, meant to draw the SAM away. They corkscrewed into the night, directly under the nose of the missile. El Sayad held his breath. *Take the bait. Take the bait...*

The missile ignored them.

El Sayad heard the pilot swear again, "I'm going to drop the bomb in five."

The drone swung far right, the SAM trailing behind it like a tail, "Four."

There was another hiss and the plant spat up a second missile. El Sayad felt sick, "Three."

El Sayad watched as the missiles grew closer, nearly touching each wing of the drone. None of his men were moving any more, eyes glued to the sky. Several of them were kneeling on the ground, praying. *Just drop the bomb, flyboy,* he wanted to shout. "Two," The pilot screamed, drifting the drone hard right. "He's gonna make it. He's gonna make it!" Someone yelled. El Sayad started praying himself.

The sky suddenly caught fire.

In a blossom of reds and yellows and oranges, the SAMs caught up. The drone exploded - a deafening fireworks display - and descended from it's perch in the air, appendages flaming like Napalm. El Sayad fell to the ground in shock, watching the aircraft spiral towards the ground gracefully. *No.*

Somewhere behind him, a soldier screamed. The chattering sound of machine guns began directly after, as if on cue. He heard grunts, yells, howls of pain from his men. El Sayad turned around dazedly. This was all a dream. It had to be.

Walking calmly down the dune was a line of uniformed men, helmeted faces illuminated by the spits of fire following each deadly blaze of bullets from their guns. They crumpled his soldiers like dying spiders. El Sayad felt his body jerk back as he was shot twice in the chest himself. An icy feeling spread from his toes to his hairline, freezing his thoughts, congealing his tongue. No one would be left standing, he knew. There would be no survivors. Gasping for breath, for life, El Sayad wondered again why he wasn't still in Paris enjoying fine alcohol and even finer women. He prayed to Allah that's where he was going. Back to France. Back to warm nights. Warm bodies.

Maybe his soul would soar over the Seine.

And haunt the Eiffel tower.

* * *

Standing on the dune, Ali Kemal flipped open his cell phone and dialed a number.

"It is done," he said quietly, "You may proceed." He nodded in agreement to whatever the person on the other end had to say, "Oh, yes. They're in for a surprise. *Salaam*, my friend."

Smirking, Ali hung up, dialed a new number and put the phone to his ear, "Mr. Clevenger. Yes. It's done. Put your fuel cells on the market. That's right. Now. You're welcome, Mr. Clevenger. Anytime."

NEW YORK CITY, NEW YORK

Director Mark Clevenger sat at the head of the conference table, staring at the blank plasma screen TV mounted on the wall behind it, his face ashen, his eyes hollow. The mug of coffee beside his hand had been exchanged for a bottle of tequila and was cold now; cold so that the grounds and the water had begun to separate. But Clevenger didn't care. He didn't care about anything anymore. SoftFuel was dead. His baby had suffocated: sat on by the IU. He had been tricked.

Screwed over by an assassin.

Clevenger swore for the thousandth time that night and pounded the table with his fist. He groaned. Ali Kemal had lied to him. The IU has been destroyed, he said over the phone. The plant has been bombed. *You've done it old boy, so put those fuel cells on the market.* And Clevenger had. That very day, before the news of any attack on the IU, he immediately began the mass production of his fuel cells and had held a press conference, announcing the maiden voyage of his new energy source. It had all gone as he had predicted. He was a genius. A visionary. His name would surely go down in the history books.

And then news of the attack on the Iranian Unity smashed into the headlines, three days later.

A failed *attempt at destroying half of the world's oil.*

Naturally, the IU declared war on the UAE. The tabloids and political analysts gave the war a week, maybe two, before the UAE joined the ranks of countries assimilated by the Unity. The Middle East was going to hell in a hat box, they all agreed. It was only a matter of time now before the other non-Unity countries gave in.

But that wasn't important to Clevenger. The IU had done exactly what they did to any new competition. *Anytime a new fuel source or oil retrieval technique comes into play, the IU lowers their prices dirt cheap so that no one wants to buy the more expensive energy source. Eventually, the alternative fuel company goes out of business and then the oil prices shoot right back up without the competition. Classic.*

His own words teased him.

He had lost several billion dollars off of this venture. SoftFuel was bankrupt. His fuel cell technology would now join the legions of others like it - collecting dust on shelves - until the world ran out of black gold. Clevenger felt like crying. He lifted the bottle of tequila to his mouth and drank deeply, alcohol dribbling down his chin and onto his designer tie.

Behind him, the conference room doors swung open, admitting a visitor.

Clevenger didn't even bother to turn around.

The man entered quietly, slowly, and made his way toward the mahogany table. His footsteps bounced off of the walls like 'taps': ponderously solemn and dirge-like. Sighing, the man took a seat closest to Clevenger. Mark kept his face in the bottle.

"Cigarette?"

Clevenger looked up deliberately, eyes burning. The evening half-light outlined Ali Kemal's features like chiseled stone. Mark stared at him hard, as if his piercing gaze would kill the assassin then and there, and let his mouth hang open vacantly, "You."

Ali merely held out a pack of Camels.

Clevenger didn't move.

"No?"

Silence.

Kemal smiled faintly and shoved a cigarette between his lips anyway, "Well, suit yourself. I hope you don't mind..." He lit up and exhaled a plume of smoke.

"You."

"Yes, me. Surprised to see me here?"

Ali waited patiently for Clevenger to catch up to his words. The director's mouth stayed shut. "I should think so. Then again, I'm sure you were even more surprised when you checked SoftFuel's stock this morning. It seems I lied to you, Mr. Clevenger," Ali said.

"You."

"We've established that it's me!" Kemal said irritatedly, rising from his chair, "The IU wanted you out of the equation, my friend. They want a lot of things. You're scheme killed Sabradan, gave the Unity the UAE, and decimated your corporation. All goals of our friendly neighborhood petroleum dealer. You can't win, Mr. Clevenger. Whether you like it or not, groups like the IU or OPEC will always be around."

Ali came up behind his chair and leaned into his ear. "And in the future, I suggest you check the loyalties of your contract killers."

Ali Kemal straightened up and walked back to his chair. Shakily, Clevenger lifted the tequila bottle and took a drink, never taking his eyes off of his assassin. He suddenly felt very overwhelmed. The IU had known all along. They had taken his plan and had turned it against him. He had played right into their hands. Into Kemal's hands.

Staring at his smoldering cigarette, Ali spoke, "Let us consider your options. In twenty four hours, the IU will release a thoroughly researched brief, describing the discovery of a far reaching conspiracy to frame the IU for the death of Mustafa Sabradan. The leader of this conspiracy will be fingered as one Marcus Clevenger. Inevitably, Interpol will take a deep interest in this man." He leaned forward. "A very deep interest."

Ali drew a SIG saur from his jacket and pointed in at Clevenger. He slipped his finger into the trigger guard, "The safety is off, Mr. Clevenger. You need only say the word. It would be my pleasure. As always."

Mark looked at the assassin. "You jackassed rag head," he said simply.

Ali Kemal shrugged and pulled the trigger. "If you insist."

Clevenger grunted, clutched his chest and fell forward, knocking the tequila bottle onto the ground. It shattered instantly, mixing the alcohol with the director's blood. Face plastered to the table, Clevenger groaned, eyes tight. Ali watched with veiled interest. The man groped at his life a moment longer and then laid still.

Calmly, Ali stood up. He inclined his head slightly toward Clevenger's corpse, transferred the gun to his gloved hand and proceeded to wipe his finger prints from the stock. As he walked towards the door, Kemal slipped the gun into Mark's limp hand. *Another tragic suicide.* A desperate solution for a desperate man. Ali Kemal felt pleased. Empowered. Ten feet tall. It was exquisite: the way the director's spine had arched in pain.

Beautiful. Always beautiful.

But something clattered to the ground behind him, shattering the oppressive quiet. Ali stopped at the door.

Frowning, he turned around slowly and caught sight of a remote control that had dropped from Clevenger's hand onto the granite tiling. The dead man's hand swung eerily above it, animated suddenly. Alive. His frown deepened.

The ceiling began to hiss.

The plasma screen TV flickered on, painting the dim room blue.

Ali stopped in mid-step, his heart beating his rib cage savagely. An alien feeling rippled down his spine and dropped into his stomach. Something wasn't right. Ali forced himself to remain calm, eying the television and the ceiling carefully. *You are in control of your environment. Analyze the situation. Be ready, Ali. Clear your mind.*

Four clouds of whitish gas started trickling from out of the A/C vents and Mark Clevenger's face appeared on the plasma screen. He was smiling. And alive. Two very undesirable traits, Ali thought.

"*Salaam*, my friend."

The assassin was rooted where he stood. The clouds billowed out into the room clinging to the walls and ground like a misty fog. *Nerve gas*, Ali thought. He shook his head. He had been stupid. Overly confident. His gaze shifted from the gas to the screen. Clevenger was still smiling.

"The tables have turned, haven't they. If you're seeing this Kemal, I'm dead. I die, you die. I'm not the type who forgives and forgets. They can't make a Christian out of me. Have you noticed the gas? Potent stuff, Somain. One of the most deadly nerve gases known to mankind. I'm sure that you're very familiar with this particular weapon, my friend. Your line of work requires it."

Ali knew about it. In fact, he had used Somain himself on several projects. The gas caused vomiting, paralysis, and then death. Not a pleasant way to go. His victims had screamed, they had begged for death.

Frantically, he turned and ran for the door. It was locked. He tugged at the handle, neck straining, eyes bulging.

"Yes, in case you're wondering, the door *is* locked," came Clevenger's voice, teasing him. "You will die here, Ali. You can't screw with me. A deal is a deal. I don't know why you did it, but you'll pay."

The gas was filling up the room. Ali coughed several times as he tore a strip from his jacket and pressed it to his mouth and nose. *A homemade gas mask.* Dizzy, he snatched a hand-carved chair and flung it one-handed at the windowed wall. He had to get out. He had to escape. Ali Kemal was always on the other end of a killing. This was just wrong. No one could stop him. He was invincible.

The chair shattered against the window, appendages rebounding against the unbroken glass.

"Oh," said Clevenger as if on cue, as if he was watching, "You might wanna know. The windows are plexiglass. Good luck breaking *them*. You'd have more luck battering down the door. Which is reinforced steel, by the way."

"Shut up," Ali roared, flinging a chair leg at the television. The screen exploded in a shower of glimmering shards.

Retching violently, reeling, Ali glanced around the room for another exit, eyes wild. The air was opaque with the Somain. He could barely see. His eyes burned. He had been tricked. Ali swore, tearing away his "gas mask" and vomited onto the ground. *First symptom.*

Through the dusky mist, Ali spotted the conference table and above it, a large maintenance vent. *An exit.* It had to be. He lurched forward and crawled onto the table. He vomited again, staining the mahogany, swearing through the stomach acids.

Clevenger's words echoed in his half delirious mind, *You will die here, Ali. You will die, you will die, you will die.*

Swallowing another retch, Ali scrambled to his feet and shoved his fingers into the vent grate. He wrenched at it with all his might, ignoring the sharp metal as it dug into his skin, drawing blood.

It held, stubborn.

He pulled again. And again. And again, sobbing in delirium. His gas mask had long since been forgotten.

Finally, the screw thread stripped and the vent clattered to the table. Ali coughed, feeling weak, his arms and legs like lead and flung his bleeding hands into the vent, gripping the edge. His eyes were getting heavy. *So tired, so tired. Just make it stop.*

Ali tried to heave himself up the vent, but he couldn't. He tried again, drawing himself halfway through the opening before falling heavily onto the table. His legs had frozen. It was as if someone had taken a pair of wire clippers and snipped the nerve that connected his hip to his brain. Writhing on the table, in his own vomit, Ali realized he was being paralyzed. *Second symptom.*

The wire clippers traveled up his body, snipping connections, robbing the brain of it's limbs. Ali couldn't think straight anymore. He felt his consciousness loosening it's grip on the world. *You will die here, Ali,* Clevenger whispered to him in the darkness. His eyelids closed slowly.

His body was still.

In the far distance, over the hissing, over Clevenger's voice, before he lost consciousness Ali heard the frantic squealing of a vole caught in a hawk's talons. It's spine was arched. It's blood was pooling. It writhed and struggled.

Save me, it screamed.

To this the hawk replied, *No hope. No hope.*

And emotionless, the bird shrieked and took flight.

So, Everything
Bryanna L.

19 (F) of Tennessee, USA

Rejection is complicated.
Take it lightly, but should you let it go?
So what if his look passed you by?
So what if he didn't get your joke?
So what if his lips were unaffected by your own?
Whether or not this matters, is all up to you.
Breathe and move on.
So.
So you gave him a piece of you and
he politely gave it back.
Return to sender.
Thanks, but please… no thanks.
So you showed him your heart,
but it was the wrong shade of blue.
So you're face,
a face which you're mother has always told you was beautiful,
didn't hold up to his own.
That smile,
not even a second glance, just
keep on walking.
But, let it be known, this is not the end
of the world.
This is merely the end of a pair of eyes
that could have cut into your own
but didn't find your gold flecks enlightening.
So.
So you took a lifetime getting ready for this moment
So you looked into the mirror before this moment

and so you thought you looked perfect for this moment
and so rejection took away the quiet pride you had in this moment
So what?
He was just one set of legs, arms, hands, eyes.
He was a neck, a chest, a breath
that left you gasping.
So what?
So.
Everything.

THE HUMAN SIDE OF THINGS
Helen B.

21 (F) of Ontario, Canada

It was all because of my eyes. Those eyes were what set me apart. I was only six years old, yet I knew I was different. I knew I wasn't like the other children. It's a hard enough for a little girl to have to move to a new country. But then to discover that the children in my new school would not accept me. It was just too much.

On that first day, when the teacher had asked me to introduce myself, kids sniggered the moment I opened my mouth. They didn't even let me tell them that my name was Ciara.

"She talks funny," one of the kids whispered to her friend.

"She talks like that 'cause she's from England, silly," said another, not so quietly as the first.

"No," I said, "I went to London once, but I'm from Ireland."

"What's the difference?"

It was a good thing my father wasn't there. He would have given that girl a good shouting-at. There was a big difference between English and the Irish, he said. But after the way these kids laughed at me, I knew there was no point in trying to tell them.

The teacher hushed the class, and let me continue. Da's company had moved so I had to come to Toronto. So far away from what I was used to. So far away from the place where the Fair Folk were the strongest. Not that I knew that as such a young age. I didn't know that I was connected to them, for until I came to Canada I had had only ever seen life on the human side of things.

When I was finished came the inevitable "Does anyone have any questions for Ciara?"

The girl who thought I was English raised her had. "Why are your eyes purple?"

That's right. My eyes were purple. Well, not exactly purple, but six-year-olds don't have the vocabulary to name all the different shades of purple there are. I think the best way to describe the colour of my eyes would be like red wine with a hint of violet. The girl's question confused me. I had never thought of the colour of my eyes. They were just there. It was as normal for me as it was for an Asian person to have straight black hair. So instead of answering, I just stood there. I could probably have explained why my name was spelled strangely. That in Irish language, the A would be pronounced, but for some reason it was changed to sound more English. But not my eyes. That was something that was just there.

When it came time for morning recess, I was smart enough to know that I should not ask anyone to play. I'd never even heard of some of the games they played, so what was the use? They'd only laugh at my accent, anyway. So I found a tree at the edge of the school yard. It was small bearing a red fruit that looked kind of like cherries.

"It's okay if I sit here, right?" I asked looking up into the branches of the tree. Something in me told me it didn't mind, that it would even like it if I sat there.

"Hey, look. The weird girl's talkin' to a tree!"

I gasped and looked forward. The boy pointing in my direction wasn't in my class. News of strange people travels fast in primary school. They live for exploiting things that are different, things they don't understand. And I was the perfect example of both. The perfect target for little kids.

"Why you talkin' to the tree?" the boy asked. "Trees don't talk back."

"It talks. I heard it talk."

And there was a chorus of laughter and insults.

"That girl's not just weird, she's mental."

"Did you see her eyes?"

"Yeah. Who has eyes like that?"

"Ha ha! She's so small."

"What is she, like three years old?"

"She must weigh only ten pounds."

"I do not!" I shouted. And that only made them laugh even more. "Shut up!" And then the tears came in buckets. My knees gave way, and I trembled uncontrollably.

A teacher came to break it up, but that was not to be the end of it. I had become the target, and there was no changing that.

When I was finally left alone, I looked back up at the tree. "So what's your name?" I asked it. "Hm?" Jesse, it seemed to say. "Okay. You can be my friend if that's okay." Of course it was.

And thus developed pattern from that moment on. I didn't speak when I didn't have to. They would laugh at the way I talked, or the things I said. So I became the target. I reckon every school must have at least one. You know, the kid that everyone has a turn teasing, or beating up on. The big schools must have one in every grade. Not that I knew any of this. All I knew was that I was six years old, I had no friends, and I didn't belong.

As I have said, the teachers' attempts to stop the teasing didn't help. Every day there was a snide remark, a reason to laugh at me. One day, when my teacher was not looking, someone threw a paper ball at me. That was the day that the pixies came to me and I learned what I truly was.

A few minutes after that paper ball was thrown at me, we were sent out to recess. As usual, I headed straight for Jesse. I didn't want to cry, but I couldn't help it. I was so lonely.

"Are you sad because you're all alone?" called a tinkling voice.

My eyes shot up, and I was completely awestruck. It's a Barbie, was my first thought. Mum had bought me one when we first came to Toronto. A sort of plea for me to feel better about the move. Didn't work, of course. This thing on Jesse's branch certainly did look like a Barbie, perhaps a bit smaller, and had a body like a Barbie. But Barbies did not wear tissue paper dresses of flowers and leaves, nor did they have tiny gossamer wings that were so small that any expert on flying would say that they shouldn't be able to fly. But they did.

"We saw what the other children do to you, so you can play with us if you want," said the second Barbie-like creature. "You have pixie blood, so you belong with us. Come."

Pixie blood? What was the Barbie talking about? No, not a Barbie. A pixie. Except, I hadn't heard of pixies before. I knew about fairies, elves, and goblins. Children's stories didn't get much more complicated than that. But these things called pixies certainly did look like the illustrations of fairies that were in the books I'd seen.

As I watched the pixies dancing on Jesse's branch, they said something I'll never forget. "It's only forever."

Forever. What does that mean to a sad little six-year-old? Nothing. So of course I agreed to go with them, and I didn't want to be the target anymore.

"It's just for a little while," said the flowery pixie.

Yeah, I know. It doesn't make much sense after the other one said it was only forever, but that's the way pixies work. I suppose she said that because she didn't want me to thing that I would be missing out on something, and that I would be able to return to the human side of things whenever I wanted. But only if things got better, of course. Besides, how could I resist what they offered me.

"We can visit Avalon and the Realm of Faerie."

"And let's not forget Narnia and Middle Earth."

"Narnia!" I shouted excitedly, much to the amusement of a few nearby kids. "Mummy read me that book."

"Book!" scoffed the leafy pixie. "Oh sure, it's just a book on this side. So is Middle Earth. People think those places were just made up by stuffy, old English men less than a hundred years ago. Not true. It was really pixies whispering in their ears that told them about such places."

"What about Never Land?" I asked.

"Naw." Flowery Pixie shook her head. "That guy had a bit of pixie in him. That gave him power to make up stuff on his own."

"Wow."

Leafy Pixie hopped off Joseph and fluttered down to my face. "So what do you say? Shall you come with us?"

I jumped up and shouted, "Yes!" And I smiled for the first time more than a month.

"Very well. Come this way."

So I followed them, and suddenly I was in a place where I thought I belonged. I was no longer the target who everyone thought was crazy because she talked to trees. In fact, there were tree sprites everywhere. Including Jesse.

"You have some intuition, little girl," he said when we met face-to-face for the first time. "Few have every tried to guess a tree's name, and you are the only mostly human to ever guess right."

"Really?"

"Truly, you are. Once there was a child who thought my name to be Ariel. How silly is that?"

"Very silly," I agreed, laughing.

"Darn right, child. Ariel does not live in our realm," said a voice behind me.

I whirled around and gasped. It was an elf. I could tell because her ears were long and pointed, and she had no wings. And her eyes . . .

"Yes." The elf nodded. "My eyes are as yours. In this realm, only the goblins and spriggans have brown eyes. It's best to stay away from them."

At such a young age, I thought this was the best thing that could have ever happened to me. This is what it must have been like for those all-human little people who were brought together for "The Wizard of Oz." to be surrounded by others like me. Nobody teased me, nobody laughed at me unless I was telling a joke, and nobody threw paper balls at me. Nobody threw anything at me unless it was in fun. So I stayed. Since I hadn't been trapped or stolen, part of me was always on the human side of things, but my mind stayed on the magical side of things as much as possible.

The thing you adults out there may be wondering is why I felt the need to stay. It doesn't last, right? Things do get better once you grow up. The teasing. The rejection. The isolation. But it did last. All through primary school. After a few years, I started to believe that things never would get better. A ten-year-old doesn't think in terms of, "What will my life be like when I'm thirty?" It hurt so much to be where I was on the human side of things.

I know things can get better now. For some. But does that mean I regret going with the pixies? Not at all. Every child needs a place where they can go to where they feel safe. It's just that my place was a little different. Except that after while it started to feel a little uncomfortable, and I wondered why I spent so much time with the pixies instead of being on the human side of things.

"Pixie," I said one day to Leafy Pixie as we climbed up the Misty Mountain, "why did I come here?" It was the first time I ever thought to question it. I was eleven years old.

"Isn't the view good enough?" she asked. "Didn't you say you wanted to see what everything looked like from high up?"

"Yes, I did. And it's great, but that's not what I mean."

Leafy Pixie blinked. "Then whatever do you mean?" she chimed. On the surface she was so innocent and ignorant, but she knew exactly what I meant.

"This world. This side of life!"

Leafy Pixie shrugged. "Hey, look at that. It's one of the great eagles. Isn't it magnificent?"

I sighed in frustration, and looked up at the eagle. It was magnificent. Eagles on the human side are a magnificent sight themselves. And a moment later, my question seemed to have been forgotten.

But then, a few hours later, as we prepared to return to Lothlorien, Leafy Pixie said, "No one can blame you for leaving the human side of things."

That's right. There were reasons why I left. All those horrible things the other kids did to me. The teasing. The rejection. The isolation. Those things made it okay for me to play on the Misty Mountain instead of the toboggan hill. None of those things existed in Middle-earth, so why shouldn't I want to go there? There were hundreds of children out there who suffered the way I did, yet I was the only one who left the human side of things. It never made any sense to me. What is there for us in a world where all we get is ridicule, insults, and are forced to be alone?

But I'm the one with the pixie blood, right? And the pixies came to me. And because they came to me, I knew I couldn't just sit there and watch while the other kids played with their friends and I was alone.

So I danced in the Fairy Circles, learned how to control the weather in Avalon, met Alsan in Narnia, and had Second Breakfast with Hobbits of the Shire. I saw all those wonderful places all-human people only ever get to see in books and movies, and even some places that they don't. Even so, at eleven years old, something was telling me that I should probably go back. I was changing, and there were no others on the magical side of things to help me understand it.

"No, but you can't go back!" protested Flowery Pixie, fluttering around in a panic.

"But I want to see what it's like on the human side of things," I told the pixies.

Leafy Pixie was a little more in control of herself. She was also rather devious. "If you stay with us you might get to meet a unicorn."

That did it. I stayed. Damn the changes I was going through! I would figure it out somehow. I mean, who wouldn't want to meet a unicorn? Unicorns are the most magical creatures in all the places I have been.

I was not given any sign as to when I would meet one, so I waited. I waited for two years. When I was thirteen, I still hadn't even caught a glimpse of one. It was time to question the pixies again.

"You promised me a unicorn," I said to them as we sailed to Narnia on the Dawn Treader. "Why haven't I seen one yet?"

"Oh, you haven't?" Leafy Pixie asked. She sounded surprised, but the pixie intuition in me told me she wasn't. The pixie shrugged. "They only show themselves to certain beings, I suppose. Maybe you're just not ready yet."

"But I've been here for seven years!" I wanted to shout, but held my tongue. It's dangerous to risk angering any of the Fair Folk. I knew that much at thirteen, and I knew how devious they could be. But still, I replied by saying, "So one will come when I'm ready?"

The pixie shrugged, her eyes filled with feigned innocence, and fluttered away. It left me feeling confused and conflicted. There was nothing I could do about it, though. Pixies are not exactly known for giving direct answers. I wanted to meet that unicorn so badly that I had to trust her. It's not like there's anything nearly as wonderful on the human side of things.

And then something happened, something I didn't expect. I started high school. Sure, it's the normal thing for children to do, but what did I do that was normal? High school was different somehow. Until then, I had been confined to small schools with fewer than four hundred student. On that first day of high school, though, I sat in the auditorium, and it was packed. There must have been as many kids there as there were in my primary school. There were so many that it would be impossible for them all to be the same.

And as I listened to the principal welcome us to the school, I realized that there were a thousand and one new things to learn and do on the human side of things. A lot of them would be up to me. I would get to choose the things I wanted to do. Then I would find people who wouldn't mind having a pixie girl as their friend, people who wouldn't mind that my accent was not one they heard very often. Things would get easier and not hurt as much.

After the welcoming assembly, I slipped into the bathroom to talk to the pixies. "I want to go back to stay," I told them.

But pixies don't give up that easily. This time, when I spoke to them, they got angry.

"Life can be easy, but it's not always that great for children like you."

"Don't tell us the hurt will stop, little pixie girl, 'cause it's gonna hurt a lot more if you go back to stay."

I shook my head. "No. It can't. Not here. It'll be different. I swear. Weren't you listening to the principal? There's something for all of us here."

"He was speaking to all-human children."

"He doesn't know what you are."

"He probably didn't even notice your funny eyes."

Then they were gone just as another girl walked in. I looked in the mirror, then quickly started washing my hands so the girl wouldn't think there was something wrong, while she took out a comb and fixed her hair. After a few seconds she looked at me. "Do you wear contacts?" she asked.

"No."

She raised her eyebrows and looked away.

So of course the hurt didn't stop. The hurt never stops. The pixies were right. I still suffered in all the same ways. The teasing. The rejection. The isolation. Even worse was the feeling that I couldn't do anything right. With new opportunities comes new challenges, and I was not up to those challenges. I had lost touch with what was expected on the human side of things. Maybe there is something that hurts worse than feeling alone and useless, but nothing I've ever come in contact with. What I thought to be the truth of the human side of things, it felt like the worst thing in the world.

Don't get me wrong. I did find some things I liked on the human side of things. Books and theatre. A different kind of wildlife, one that you knew would not talk back to you. But I wasn't used to all the technology, and contemporary music. The noise and the pace of the modern human world.

And it's not like I didn't find friends. I did. It's just . . . They weren't the true friends that I had hoped they would be.

So one day, I went back. Back to Jesse. "Call them," I said. "Call the pixies. I want to talk to them."

<u>All right, Ciara. Remain calm.</u> I did not so much hear the words, as I understood them.

A moment later, the pixies came.

"So, it's you," said Leafy Pixie.

"Have you decided to return to us?" asked Flowery Pixie.

"Yes," I sobbed. "I'm sorry. I'm sorry about everything I said to you. You were right. It hurts too much. None of those people are my true friends."

And the pixies were all too eager to take me back. Together they said, "Maybe in Faerie you'll find someone true."

They spoke so confidently. There was none of the trickster in their voices. I just had to believe them. It wasn't until much later that I began to realize that it was probably the most ironic thing they had ever said to me. For when I went back to Faerie, every think felt just as false, maybe even more so than the humans were. The lies they gave me were nice, and they made me feel a whole lot better. But they were still lies, and that wasn't right, not even for a pixie girl like me.

It was at the top of a mountain in Ireland that it finally became clear. "Pixies, I must go back. None of this is real."

"But it's so quiet and beautiful here. None of that loud music you hate so much," said Leafy Pixie.

"Or cars, or phones or airplanes," said Flowery Pixie.

"And look. Doesn't the moon look like a crystal?"

"There's no lie in that moon."

I couldn't agree more with that. It's warm glow could heal the soul of a lonely girl like me. The Faerie moon was one of the most beautiful things in the Realm, and it did sparkle like a crystal. But it's not the sort of crystal we think of on the human side of things. Maybe there were no lies in that moon, but it scattered pieces of truth the way a normal crystal scatters beams of light.

"I don't care! I don't care if it is true! I'm more human than pixie, and you know it! This isn't the way it's supposed to be for humans."

"But you can't go back!" protested Flowery Pixie.

"Remember the teasing?" added Leafy Pixie

"The rejection?"

"The isolation?"

"I know it's gonna hurt," I said, "but that's all a part of being human, Leafy Pixie."

"It's only forever."

"Not gonna work this time. I'm not a little girl anymore."

Not a little girl anymore . . . That's right. We all knew it, and none of us liked it. During all those games, dances, parties, feasts and adventures, something happened to me. I changed. Humans change. Pixies stay the same. I didn't belong with them any more than they belonged in a chemistry class. Leaving them was the right thing to do.

It wasn't an easy thing to do. I left the magical side, and I'm here on the human side of things to stay. It's only forever, right? No. I'm not going to stay for good. I will go back one of these days. When I get a bit older. I'll dance in a Fairy Circle, learn how to control the weather in Avalon, meet Aslan in Narnia, and have Second Breakfast with Hobbits of the Shire. Right now, though, I've got things to do on the human side of things. I've got books to read, plays to see, classes to take, and jobs to do. You know. Grown-up stuff.

It's a strange thing, really, calling the pixie girl a grown-up. I still look like a kid, giggle like a kid, and I love children's books. I wear brown contact lenses these days. I don't know if that will make it any easier, but it's a start, even if they do make me feel like a goblin at times. A grown-up is what I am now, and there are certain things grown-ups do.

Even so, no matter what happens, I am going to meet that unicorn for real one day.

ANGELS DWELL IN HARMONY
R. J. Simmons

22 (M) of Oregon, USA

Were we the last of twilight to succumb,
forever something to become -
shameless of the reckless wheel,
spinning still an eternal deal.
We are masters of our fate,
witching hour inside the gate,
ignore the magic or just wait?

The whitest glow, the purest blunder
spiteless now of Kali's hunger -
a temper tempest worthy of Thor's thunder.
The ox's eyes have not a wonder;
would be a shame for love to sunder.

Angels dwell in harmony,
no need for plated armory.
Cupid with his twisted archery -
once inside it strikes an artery,
revealed as a radiating Valkyrie.

So spin the wheel of fortune,
set the hooded demons arm in motion,
if only there were such a potion,
skin smoother than from any lotion.
The brightest pearl in all the ocean.

My ancestry digs the grave,
not even a shovel allowed the knave.

The jack of spades acutely taught,
thirty silver and Judah's bought.
To live again as life is fear,
in your soul I'll find that tear,
with my reflection in the mirror.

LIGHT LIKE LIFE
Tim A.

17 (M) of New South Wales, Australia

Light, spent all its worth for the day, lost to a maniacal moon, hell bent on spreading long skeleton-like shadows across the steps of each front porch.

But my city lies dreaming.

Creeps, crooks and scoundrels bring destruction a sidewalk away from blissfully sleeping families. They do it not for the money, nor for the high. They do it because, in this city, my city, it's the easiest trade to learn. Guns, drugs and a low profile, the three things people like that understand and relate to. They think they go unnoticed, and to an extent, they do. But they don't get passed me, these eyes, these broken dilated pupils strain through each night watching them continue their desecration of what I built.

This was a quiet suburban town when I first moved here. Dreams, ideas and a briefcase full of good intentions. But that was some 40 years ago now. Don't get me wrong, there was a time I had gotten everything right, my dreams stood as they do today, only they were the benchmarks of change, these buildings excited and drew people in. I changed everything here. Maybe I changed a little too much.

I looked down at my blunt battered hands. My pulse more visible than usual, I'd come to take interest in the way the flow of my blood connected with the thoughts that flowed through my head. It gave me one more thing to ponder. As if I needed another.

My eyes once again adjusted to the scenery from my penthouse balcony, and allowed me to gaze upon my city the way Dr. Frankenstein would have as he watched his monster defy him and the work he had done.

The sun once streamed through the main street creating long distinct shadows on the sidewalk chasing in vain the true version of the form they are seen in.

It's amazing what 4 decades, $50 billion and this overzealous mayor can do to a city.

I drew this city into the age of darkness, with promises and ideas built 150 stories into the sky. Scrapers and towers made us nocturnal, made us fear, made us afraid of the streets we once embraced.

Year after year I am forced to re-evaluate my intentions for running this disgusting cesspool of filth that sickens me to the very pit of my being. But every year I come to the same conclusion, every year the families vote because they know not of what goes on and the criminals vote because they know I cannot beat them. So I don't stand down, but I don't take up arms.

In my earlier years I had recurring nightmares of a world very distant to that of which I belonged. Where a crime was to love and not let go, where buildings were better abandoned than restored, where the air was so thick and chalky that it left a foul taste on the tongues of all that inhaled it. Everything was dull and brown as if it was printed in sepia tones, every fire could not be put out, every window remained broken and every war could not be stopped.

Sometimes I dreamed I was inside a plastic bubble as it melted, suffocating me with every forced breath of its toxic air. I would try and scream but all I would hear was the muffled laughter of an auditorium full of people, watching as my lungs scorched with the pain of a thousand lost loves vanished in an instant.

These images stained my head with worry. Every night I would offer my soul for half hour increments to put off the inevitable. I prayed to my friends to not let me sleep. A promise they couldn't keep, as night after night I was met with the usual sepia world until one day. I woke up in it.

It wasn't a gradual thing; at least I don't think it was. The nights around then just blur together in my mind. For all I know, I fell asleep one night, I dreamt, and I woke up like this. The longer time drifted away from that morning I've wondered whether or not I actually did wake up. Wondering If I'm just paralysed here in an imaginary nightmare like some painful coma, if someone is sitting by my hospital bed whispering sadistic tales of murder and bloodshed, of a city gone mad, with no means of salvation.

I shuffled my way back into the apartment and sat down at my desk. The padded leather frame I moulded in to had been my counterpart through everything. That one chair had watched me silently as I made every decision that had influenced the rise and plummet of this city.

I'd spent hours spinning a pen around my with my index and middle fingers debating. Its strange how I needed hours upon hours to change a parking violation code or to add a pedestrian crossing here or there, but for a decision of such catastrophic consequences, tonight, my mind was already made up.

I opened the bottom draw and retrieved a small stack of papers I'd been putting off for a while now. Nothing different to the usual legal prattle I had to go through each and every day. Just lately I hadn't felt like anything I approve, anything I change can have a positive impact on the world I created outside my window. After all, this is how it all began. I sat down at this very desk, took out a pen, and approved everything. I wanted things to change. I wanted everything to change. Now I'd give anything to have that chance again.

So just like all those other times, I took out my pen, and I signed, I signed not in hope of any improvement. Just so I could feel as if I'd never given up trying. To me, my name meant nothing but a title, but to this city, it meant approval, it meant evolution. I can't remember the last time I signed my name without feeling the pressure of if I didn't cross that last 't'.

I finished up and took a last glance out the large glass windows surrounding me, strolled out of my office, and retreated to the lobby.

I stepped foot onto the shabby concrete sidewalk of my urban, modern day ghost town as my memory clicked through old images of each corner of each street like a slide show. I often enjoyed these long walks home, but this night I felt uneasy the whole trip, I felt as if the towns' eyes traced my every footstep with dreaded insecurities.

My head knew they were sleeping but the beating of my heart told me everyone knew. I was a bullet away from infamy, although that never occurred to me at the time.

I counted each of the 4021 steps it took to reach my front gate despite the constant wandering of my mind. It was something I had always wanted to know, it was a night of last chances.

When I arrived in my library everything was in place as I had left it. It resembled an empty disaster film set waiting for the call of 'action'.

My beautiful mahogany bookshelf had recently toppled spilling Hemingway and Melville across the magnificent marble floor.

I turned away from the scene that lay before me and entered the kitchen. Pots and pans stacked the sink almost high enough to reach the distant ceiling. I had stopped doing them when I discovered the news. I was decaying, rotting slowly from the inside, ravished by age and a trace of lung cancer. Poisoned by the same thing that destroyed my city. Alcohol and cigarettes, both of which I am responsible for bringing to this town, so I guess, I indirectly brought this onto myself.

I watched my skin sag, felt my head drown in thoughts of extinguishing itself, all this time whilst my city, my one true possession, began to whither away to nothing.

Maybe my city is getting its revenge on me? Maybe this is its way of declaring independence? Maybe it was never my city at all? Maybe I'm just a fool, a ship too proud to ever sink.

Bending down to pull open the stove I let out a deep heart aching cough that echoed through the 32 rooms of this house. I placed my head into the oven and slowly turned the gas knob on. The smell hit me instantly so I stepped back watching as the light shining from the lamp above me bent and twisted through the heavy gas as it lifted itself from the stove and floated through my house.

I allowed the stove door to remain open and quietly stepped into the library checking that all the windows seen on the way between the two rooms were closed so that no air could escape. I quietly retreated to my favourite chair, comforted by the faint squeak it let out as I reclined back to my favourite position. I leaned over the edge of the chair and picked up my new first edition copy of "A Farewell to Arms".

Hemingway made me feel safe in my own skin, no man quite brought problems onto himself like Hemingway, and he produced some special things. I always thought I could do the same despite everything I put myself and these people through.

How fitting we should meet a similair fate.

By now I could feel the gas slipping in and out of my lungs, leaving more and more carbon monoxide in the pits of my stomach each time. I shook last thoughts out of my head and returned to my book.

It took a while for my eyelids to begin to droop, but it was soon over. My head fell back onto the cushion I had strategically placed, and I drifted off to sleep.

And you know what?

The nightmares were over.

AND THEY SAY FAIRYTALES DON'T COME TRUE
Via M.

19 (F) of Ohio, USA

"This is the last box," Paul declared with a serious sigh of relief. The cardboard box plopped down on the hardwood floor on the foyer, next to twenty of its twin brothers and sisters. The boy wiped his forehead as he entered a kitchen filled with only more of the boxes closest friends—and a slightly older woman unpacking them.

She turned to Paul and smiled sweetly, though he seemed much less enthused, "Good! Thanks sweetie." She went on about her business, unpacking things and putting them on cabinets and in cupboards. The kitchen was full of light that afternoon, though the lack of curtains or shades certainly didn't stop the sun in the least. Paul squinted in the sunlight, glancing out to the street at the kids playing. His brow furrowed, as if in deep thought, though he never spoke. His mother turned her attention back to him, "Oh, by the way! One of our new neighbors came over a little while ago. She is having a little get-together tonight and she invited us over, it starts at four-thirty."

Paul sighed before moving his gaze back to her. He turned up one side of his mouth and lifted his brows in a begging form, "...do we *have* to go?"

"Yes we *have* to go. Come on, this will be good! Maybe you'll meet some kids that go to your school! It'll be fun."

Paul crossed his arms and smiled slightly, nodding only to please his mother—truth was he didn't care if he never met his neighbors, things like that were just awkward for him. His mother shuffled quietly across the floor and stood before him, placing her hands on his elbows, "Hey, everything's going to be okay here, okay? I promise." Her face was reassuring, as were her fingertips as she moved a piece of Paul's shaggy curls from his eyes. Only a short moment passed before she broke the silence once again, "Now go get cleaned up, the box of soap and things should be in the bathroom." She moved back to her boxes and Paul exited the kitchen and headed up the stairs to honor his mother's wishes.

* * *

As four-thirty came around, the pair made their way down the sidewalk to the dinner party a few houses down with a bowl of pasta in their hands. The house was huge, four or five stories at least. It was very straight up, though, much thinner than the rest of the houses on the block. It was definitely an odd house which Paul quickly concluded would be creepy in the dark. There were several noises from the back of the house: a splash here and there, feminine laughs, low music.

Suddenly, a louder shrieking noise came their way, "Yoohoo! Caroline! Come on back!" The two turned their heads to see a frantic woman dressed in nearly all white, all the way up to her hat, waving them over with one hand and holding a drink in the other.

Caroline waved back and they headed that direction. Paul raised a brow to her and whispered from the corner of his mouth, *"You owe me big time."*

As they entered the back yard they were met with a sea of bright colors, so much so Paul felt he had to squint just to look about. A lavished pool full of small children in bright bathing suits was surrounded by white tables, one full of women who seemed to be nearly carbon copies of the woman who met them at the gate.

She, Debora, was talking a mile and minute while introducing Paul and Caroline to the ladies of the table. Paul, though, wasn't really listening. He was, instead, wondering where all the men were. He appeared to be the only teenager present as well. The three of them joined the ladies but they stuck out, Paul and Caroline being the only two not in white or some off-white substitute.

Paul's attention was rudely jerked to the scene at hand as he heard his name, "So, Paul, how hold are you?"

He turned to the woman and smiled a little, pretending to be grateful that she was acknowledging him, "Seventeen."

"Junior? Senior?"

"Senior this year."

She nodded, but didn't really know what else to say to him. Thankfully, she didn't have to as Debora took over for her, "Oh, I have a daughter your age!" She was excited, smiling, leaning up as she spoke.

Caroline jumped in, "Oh? Does she go to West Hamilton?"

There was an awkward silence. Debora lost her smile, the other women nervously moved their gaze to their laps or their drinks—it didn't take a genius to figure out something was up.

Debora's answer was quiet, though definable, "No, no she doesn't." She moved her chair back and grabbed her half-full glass, "I'm out of wine! Excuse me." She excused herself and left the group.

It took only a few seconds after Debora was gone from sight for one of the women to comment, "It's a shame about their little girl."

Paul and Caroline just stared blankly at the woman, awaiting an explanation for the new people. As the woman turned to them, she realized she must explain, though she didn't right away—it was apparent that she liked to feel superior. She took a sip of her wine and took her time placing it back down before leaning back in her chair to tell her story, "Poor girl, she had a case of food poisoning so bad it attacked her entire system and left her in a coma; been that way for over a year now. I told Deb not to buy those apples from that ghastly vendor she insisted on." She lost track of her thoughts for a moment, popping back in as if she never trailed in the first place, "Well, anyway, she's here at the house. I hear she's hired seven different nurses now to care for her, two for each shift and one constantly on call. It's sad, really, she just can't let go."

Caroline nodded and glanced at Paul, offering just a small bit of input; enough to be concerned but not too much to seem as butting in, "That *is* sad." Paul and Caroline's eyes connected, and there was something else going on behind them besides a general concern for this girl neither of them knew.

The chatting woman noticed the odd silence between them, "Oh, I'm sorry...you probably didn't need to know that."

The pair snapped out of their trance and turned to her, Caroline offering a limited amount of info for an explanation, "Oh no, it's okay. It's just...my husband, he was in a coma, he just passed."

Before the other women even had time to throw their sympathetic remarks their way, Paul stood up, "I'm going to use the restroom." He lingered for a moment, just long enough to be told where it was, and left for the house. On his way out he heard his mother's voice addressing the group quietly, *"He's having a hard time with it."* He shook his head, though continued on.

Once inside the home, he was struck by what to do. He didn't *actually* need to use the restroom, he just needed an excuse to leave. There were voices coming from the kitchen; Paul slid by it stealthily and made his way up a flight of stairs. At the top he was met with a very small hallway with another set of stairs at the other end. A shiver ran down Paul's spine; something was just creepy about this place. There were photos all over the walls between the lights, all the staircases were rounded, and the whole place seemed abnormally dark. But still, Paul felt more comfortable being in the home than outside faced with a million questions from people he barely knew.

There were family photos lining the walls as he climbed the next set of stairs. He recognized Debora in all of them, though there was an older man and a little girl in them as well who Paul assumed were her husband and daughter. He turned his attention to the stairs below his feet as he went up another level in the home. The stairs creaked with every step, making Paul a tad uneasy but he didn't stop—he liked exploring.

Finally, he reached a hallway that lacked another set of stairs at either end. Paul had no idea what floor he was on by this point, other than it was the top one. Suddenly, a glimpse of light caught his eye at the back end of the hall—an open door. He slowly made his way down the hall to the door and wrapped a hand around the edge of it, pushing it open slowly with a creak. The sun spilled into the room from two large windows enough that it nearly blinded Paul. He had to shut the door and stand behind it just to move out of the light path. As his vision became clearer he took in the room; but, mainly, the girl in the middle of it.

Placed upon a bed of white cotton—well, as white as hospital bed linens could be—lay a young girl Paul's age. She had brilliant creamy, pale skin adorned with short hair so dark it could almost be black. She was covered with a white sheet up to her shoulders, leaving only the tee shirt she wore showing above it. There were flowers all over the room as if to simulate an outdoor experience while indoor. On the wall behind her bed wooden letters spelled out "SHELBY" as large as could be. Paul wondered if she had done that herself, or if that was an addition made by her mother.

He had a hard time breaking his stare from the beautiful young woman, but he felt he needed too. He strolled about the room and investigated the trophies, pictures, and framed certificates strategically placed in every possible nook. He picked up a picture of just Shelby, an almost candid but she happened to look just at the right time. Paul's hazel hues instantly connected with Shelby's chocolate spheres in the photo, and for the first time in a long time he cracked a sincere smile. He set the picture back down in its respective spot and wandered over to Shelby's bedside.

She was the most stunning creature Paul had ever seen. He could almost feel the warmth of her eyes behind her closed lids. Her beautiful locks blew lightly in the wind entering from the window. Her soft, perfectly red lips were slightly pursed as if there were a tart taste behind them. Paul stroked the slender digits on her hand lightly before whispering so low he couldn't even hear himself, *"If I could I would make you mine."*

A soft, soothing wind blew in through the window as he gentle kissed the tip of his finger and touched it to the perfect lips of the sleeping girl. He smiled one last time to her and turned to leave the room.

"….did you save me?" A soft, almost inaudible voice came from behind him. He whirled around fast as lightning to see Shelby lying on the bed with her eyes wide open. He stumbled backwards, running into a chest of drawers and causing a disturbance signaling the arrival of two nurses—one of which immediately shoved him out of the room and slammed the door shut.

Paul just stood still outside the door for a moment trying to reply the whole thing in his head…*did that really just happen?* He shook his head and once he regained the ability to move his legs he turned and ran all the way down the five floors and into the backyard, screamed a loose 'I gotta go' across the yard and took off down the street.

It is said that Shelby White had a full recovery, finished high school, graduated college, but has never been married. Pau Charmingl, however, to this day has never again set foot in the White's home or within a fifty foot radius of Shelby—he has never married either. Some say Shelby moved back to her family's estate and spends her days in her room at the top of the home just waiting for her Prince Charming to come whisk her away.

NOTES IN A DORMITORY
Lisa K.

17 (F) of Connecticut, USA
Down beats the second hand: meter
of functioning life in this place where
all the world gets ready to
articulate onto fine A2s
the notes to get them through the day.

She is a messenger, who
marches con-nun-drumming-ly along
to tail the memos to doors; who watches
the strings between notes wind,
as the day progresses,
a carpet under her feet to hold her balance.
But no matter the note, each strand avoids
that space in the middle of the hall: the hole
where everyone stops to breathe.

AN ART OF DECEPTION
Lyndsey M.

17 (F) of Texas, USA

There was a quiet field in Sussex that was once used for grazing cows. Years after the owner passed away and the barn was destroyed, the paddock stood alone, and the meadow served little purpose. There was, however, one week every year when a carnival came to the small field, drawing crowds from all the surrounding counties.

A number of tents were set up along the moors, strung together with lines of triangular flags, languidly flopping in the wind. Visitors weaved through a coin toss, a house of mirrors, a circus, a cake walk, and a number of strange demonstrations. In one corner stood a large (but slightly lopsided) tent with a sign that read HOUSE OF MARVELS. Its show times were listed below the title in crooked lettering. Just beyond the pinned-back flap of the tent sat a man named Mr. Weatherby. He was watching his assistant, Cornelius, fumble with a glass bottle as he attempted to pry the cap off with his teeth.

Mr. Weatherby could never remember exactly where he had found Cornelius. Quite frankly, Mr. Weatherby did not care. The young man was fairly quiet, and he had no distinguishing qualities besides a lack of personal finesse. It seemed that his bowler hat was always askew, and the copper buttons of his frock coat never matched up. It was a pity, Mr. Weatherby thought. He might have been quite handsome, had he paid more attention to presentation. But the important thing was that he rarely asked questions. Mr. Weatherby did not like answering questions.

He turned his attention to a scholarly-looking man touring the exhibit, who was presently bent over the show's newest asset, an ancient Egyptian mummy in an open sarcophagus. The case was gilt with shimmering hieroglyphics that glimmered in the half-light of the tent.

"It's real," said the man, stroking his chin.

"Of course it's real," said Mr. Weatherby. "Couldn't believe my luck when I came across it. I don't think I've seen anything like it. Neither had Cornelius - had you, son?"

Cornelius replied that he had not.

The scholarly man nodded and moved on. Mr. Weatherby suppressed a sigh of relief. Had the stranger been a *touch* more educated, he might have noticed that the exhibit was quite similar to one that had recently gone missing from the Czartoryski Museum. Strikingly similar.

All coincidence, of course.

The exhibit also included a pen of miniature ponies (those were real), the bow of Robin Hood (that wasn't), a painting by Titian (that was real), and the sword of Hiero II of Syracuse (which Mr. Weatherby had *thought* was real until he noticed that a particularly sibylline Roman had engraved the blade to congratulate Hiero's efforts in the *First* Punic War). Equally impressive (and equally questionable) artifacts, plants, and animals filled the other displays.

"It's a very impressive collection," said the man, who, to Mr. Weatherby's dismay, had not left yet – after customers paid their pennies, he usually did his best to hurry them along. "But you don't have much from Southern Asia. You should look into a few pieces from India or Bangladesh, that neck of the woods, you know?"

Mr. Weatherby stroked his chin. "You think so?"

"Absolutely. A rarity like that would give you a very well-rounded collection. Most profitable, I'm sure."

Mr. Weatherby raised an eyebrow.

* * *

The Bengal Tiger exhibit was eerily quiet at night. The entire zoo took on a sinister shade at this hour. Moonlight glinted off the chain link fences and played in Mr. Weatherby's dark eyes as he surveyed the situation.

"Please tell me you didn't forget the dart gun," said Mr. Weatherby. Cornelius stared blankly at him. "You haven't forgotten it, have you?"

Cornelius, pulling the gun from his burlap sack, replied that he had not.

Mr. Weatherby pulled the gun from Cornelius' grip and tucked it underneath his arm. Cornelius followed close behind. They crept along the outer wall of the tigers' pen, silently watching the velvety fur of the sleeping animals rise and fall with their breathing. As they reached the gate, Mr.

Weatherby pulled a brass chatelaine from his pocket. He tried several dainty silver keys in the lock before one of them finally clicked, and he gently pulled the lock from its chain and handed it to Cornelius. Mr. Weatherby pushed the door ajar, and the two men filed in quietly. Mr. Weatherby stood for a moment, gazing at the majestic felines.

Suddenly, Cornelius dropped the padlock. It made a sharp clinking sound against the gravel, and one animal's head lifted up, ears perked.

"Cornelius!" Mr. Weatherby hissed, turning to glare at the youth. "Do you have any semblance of a brain at all?"

Cornelius replied that he had not.

Mr. Weatherby sighed. "Hand me the gun. I'll have to tranquilize all of them now. I must admit, you do have a penchant for bringing out the worst in a scenario." Cornelius handed him the equipment and backed away a few paces. Mr. Weatherby sited his target, licking his lips. "Say, Cornelius, you didn't give me any darts." He paused. "Cornelius?" He turned, and his mouth slowly fell open.

Cornelius stood outside of the tiger pen, reattaching the padlock to the thick metal chain that held the gate closed. He was whistling a section from one of Mendelssohn's concertos.

"Cornelius, surely this is some sort of joke. "

The young man shook his head.

"Cornelius," he said, his voice tinged with desperation, "haven't you ever had one ounce of sympathy for me? One morsel of it?"

Cornelius, happily jingling the keys, replied that he had not.

MY SMILING ROSE
Mary B.

16 (F) of Missouri, USA

The hospital smelled like turpentine and Band-aids. I drummed my fingers impatiently on the elevator wall as the dull, yellow buttons slowly dinged their way up to the fifth floor. John was up there, and I needed his strong hand to squeeze my own in reassurance that he would be coming home the next day.

I smiled; he would love the *Journey's Greatest Hits* CD I had brought him. One of the things that attracted me to him was our shared love of '80's rock. My mom constantly joked about how we belted out the songs she blasted on her radio in high school, but that didn't bother us. "Don't Stop Believing" was the greatest song ever created, and "Faithfully" was "our" song.

I hummed "Open Arms" under my breath as I made my way to the nurses' unit.

"Excuse me," I said, "could you tell me where room 512 is?"

A redheaded woman glanced over her shoulder, chomping her bright pink gum like tar. "Sure, hon," she drawled. "Fourth room on the right down this hall." She jabbed her finger toward the left.

I braced myself as I stood outside the honey-colored door. The last time I had been in a hospital was when my Grandma Addy had died; I hadn't been to one since. John was different, though—*he* was coming home.

I rapped twice before I barreled into the room. "John!" I called out excitely. "Look what-"

I stopped abruptly. That—that shriveled thing wasn't my boyfriend.

I buried my face in my hands. She was so tiny, just like Grandma had looked on that ocean of white sheets. I choked down a sob. "M'am," I croaked, "I-I'm so sorry! I thought this room was my boyfriend's."

Her head lethargically rotated in my direction. Fixing her wan, blue eyes on my face, she mumbled, "What—you leavin', too? Only Johnny stays with ol' Patsy, God bless him." She faced the window again, a single tear trickling down her right cheek.

I couldn't just leave her. She even had Grandma's snub nose.

I covered the distance to her bed in three steps. Grasping her wrinkled hand, I reached up and smoothed her sparse white hair from her forehead.

"It's okay," I murmured, stroking her hand gently, "I'll stay."

She slowly turned toward me again, disbelief etched on her face. "You-you'd do that?" she whispered, eyes shining with tears. I nodded briefly and squeezed her hand again. Her gaze traveled over my face, finally resting on my own hazel eyes. Dimpling, she squeezed my hand back.

"Johnny must have sent you," she whispered.

"Who?" I raised my eyebrows.

"Johnny, my husband."

"Oh, I-"

"Don't worry, sweet," she said. "Johnny's been gone near a year." She stared wistfully into the distance. "Married sixty years, we were, and every bit of it full of roses—red roses, mind you."

"Oh!" I cried. "I *love* red roses!"

For the first time, her eyes sparkled. "Can you imagine getting one every *day?*" she asked, grinning and revealing a chipped front tooth. "Johnny never missed a day throughout our marriage."

"How beautiful!" I murmured. "I'd marry someone in an *instant* if they did that for me."

"Oh, sweet, not an *actual* red rose every day!" She chuckled. "Johnny said his love for me was like a red rose---poignant, passionate, and enduring. He told me the night of our honeymoon that he would do something for me every day in our marriage that represented those three things." A quavering smile snaked onto her face, and she looked at me through filmy eyes. "He called them our red roses, and they meant more to me than any flower." She stifled a sob and gently squeezed my hand.

I don't know how long I knelt there beside her. Nothing needed to be vocalized; our eyes did that. When I finally thought I heard even breathing, I gently slipped my hand from hers. Lightly brushing my lips across her forehead, I turned toward the door, but I felt a slight tug on my pink shirt.

Her eyes smiled into mine. "Thank you for being my red rose today," she whispered. Finding my hand, she gripped it gently one last time.

Her eyes weren't so wan anymore.

With one last smile, I slipped out the door and shut it gently behind me. I didn't even realize I had started walking until the bubble-popping nurse's voice jolted me out of my reverie.

"Have a nice visit?" she boomed. "Ol' Patsy can be a handful." She winked roguishly.

"A-actually," I stammered, slightly blushing, "I went into the wrong room. I was looking for my boyfriend's room, but I think I got the numbers mixed up. Is there anyone in room 521?"

The nurse guffawed. "Why, *is* there? The whole staff's been "ooing" and "aahing" ever since he got here yesterday!" She slapped the desk as if it was the funniest thing she'd heard all day.

I forced a smile. "Is it down the same hall?"

"Yup," the nurse replied, popping another piece of gum into her mouth and winking. "Be sure to give him a kiss for me!"

Her laughter reverberated throughout the hall as I sped down to 521. Not even bothering to knock, I burst in and ran smack into John. Stumbling backwards, I fell down on my backside, a shocked look on my face.

John almost fell over laughing. "Do that again," he gasped between snorts, "and the nurses won't let me come home tomorrow!"

I scrambled up and flung my arms around his neck. Leaning on his crutch, he clung tightly to me with his free arm and buried his face in my hair.

"Mmm," he murmured, playing with my locks and gazing deep into my eyes. "Good."

I traced the logo on the front of his polo shirt. "I brought this for you," I announced, holding up the plastic CD over and kissing him on the nose.

He grinned and kissed it with a French flair. "This is almost as good as the surprise I have for you," he said with a conspiratorial wink.

I gasped. "You have something for *me*? Oh, show me, John, show me!"

He laughed and grabbed my hand. "Only if you promised to keep your eyes shut," he taunted playfully.

"Oh, I *suppose* I can," I replied with an exaggerated sigh.

We slowly hobbled to his bedside, my hand entwined in his. "Wait here," his hot breath expelled in my ear, sending pleasant shivers down my spine.

After a few seconds, I felt something long and tapering pressed into my hand. "You can open your eyes now!" he chirruped excitedly.

I slowly unveiled my eyelash curtain. Jerking backwards, I gasped and threw my hand over my mouth.

"Oh-my-"I murmured, salty tears stinging my cheeks.

John enveloped me in a hug as his eyes darted over my face. "Did I do something wrong?" His voice dripped with concern, but all I could do was mutely shake my head.

I stroked the satin petals absentmindedly. Suddenly, I faced him and gripped his hand—*hard*.

"John," I said, my voice tight with emotion, "I met someone today."

I told him the whole story of "Ol' Patsy." By the time I was finished, tears were streaming down his face, too, Letting out a hoarse cry, he pulled me into a hug so tight I thought I wouldn't ever be able to breathe again.

"Mel," he said, tightly clutching the folds of my shirt, "that lady is my grandma."

I clapped my hand over my mouth. "*What?*" I asked incredulously.

He smiled and stroked my cheek with his thumb. "She's told that story so many times I could say it in my sleep. She's the one I told you about who's progressing steadily in Alzheimer's. She-she's never forgotten that story, a-and I know she never will." He let out a strangled sob and buried his face in my hair.

We sat there for a long time, just rocking back and forth and spilling years' worth of tears about our loved ones. Finally, John cradled my face gently in his hands and gave me an Eskimo kiss.

"Thank you so much for making her happy," he murmured, "just like you make me." He folded our hands over the rose.

"See this?" he asked, nodding toward the rose with his head. "You're getting one every day."

I nestled my head into his chest. "Guess what?" I whispered. "I know what *my* rose is today."

A puzzled look crossed his face. "Yeah, I just gave-"

"No," I interrupted, tapping his nose with my finger. "You."

He just smiled.

SONG OF SOLOMON
Morgan H.

17 (F) of Georgia, USA
Breaking your sound barrier with words
you can't comprehend and you don't fit any more
because you don't fit.
You've tried to squeeze yourself with effort,
but after a while, it starts to hurt
and the secrets placed in your 8th grade notebooks offer
a sort of solemn antithesis to your current state.
You fight back the tears inside where all your memories lie,
trampled over and forgotten at the very bottom of your soul.
You used to read Shakespeare
because you wanted
it from yourself.

Sitting in a cold white room staring at the pictures on the wall.
I know how you feel.
And it must've hurt to watch your world flushed down a gutter
in the light pitter patter of rain we had last spring. You tried
to convince yourself of things impossible
and admittedly, you made it. But now you're watching
as a piece of concrete chinks across faded sidewalk-cracked and jagged-

and your hands slip down your side in the exact way
hers did. It must've stung to know
your perfection (invincibility) was as real
as her love for computers.

Do you remember the sound of autumn and the
sacred whispers of winter?
Do you remember the apathy we felt for another
year of high school and all the clamor of home room?
Was the sound of chalk on blackboards a sort of
lace reminder that you didn't know everything there was to know?
Do you miss the way the chem lab smelled?
Does the sound of bells ring in your ears?
Is another year of high school enough?
Do you feel the apathy growing?
Do you feel it?
Do you feel it?
It's here...

I miss you.

SCOTCH ON THE ROCKS
Donovan J.

21 (M) of California, USA

"I'll have a scotch." The bar was empty this time of night: at eight o' clock, post meridiem, most of the pub-hoppers hadn't yet arrived. A few men sat at the bar, the hardcore drunks, who arrived before dusk and left only when kicked to the curb in the wee hours of the morning.

The bartender plucked a small, squat glass from behind the counter with a lazy but practiced grab and set it on the counter. "How d'you want it, Kiddo?" Earl always called him that–Kiddo. From the first day Mike had met the aging bartender, nearly a year earlier, he'd called him that. Maybe it was because he was always the youngest guy in the bar when he walked in the door at eight o' clock, sharp. Maybe it was because he looked as though he was still in high school. Maybe the old man just liked him. Whatever the reason, it was always with a smile. Mike liked that about Earl.

"On the rocks," he said, sliding his money across the counter. They'd been through this cycle dozens of times–Mike put the actual number in the low three hundreds. Since the start of their odd friendship, Earl's words, and Mike's replies to them, had remained unchanged.

Earl's hand came from behind the bar holding a bottle filled with the amber fountain of youth. Earl was a practical man. He did not attempt to spin the bottle on the flat of his palm, nor did he try to pour the glass from a ridiculous height. He swiftly overturned it, dumping its contents into the glass, which had, as if by magic, been filled with three cubes of ice. When it was full, almost to the brim, he slid it back to Mike with his fingertips without spilling a drop. Nevertheless, he still wiped the counter down with a damp cloth afterward.

"Thanks Earl."

"No problem, Kiddo." There it was again. Mike wondered if the old man even knew his name. "Where you been? We missed you last night."

Mike chuckled. "Well, ah...I was out."

Then it was Earl's turn to let out a haughty laugh. "Kiddo, the only place you go...is here."

The twenty-two year old Philosophy major felt his face flush red. He took a small sip of his scotch, letting the holy liquid sizzle in his mouth a moment before sending it tumbling down his throat.

"Ah...true enough," he said with a helpless smile. A moment passed, with no words between the two. These silences were not uncommon, but they were not uncomfortable in the least. It was more akin to the silence of a library–like minds in an atmosphere they enjoy.

Mike took a second sip of his scotch.

"So–who's the girl?" Mike glanced up to see the bartender staring intently at him, wiping down a glass with his damp cloth in the classic barkeep pose. Mike felt his cheeks burning.

"Ah...well, funny story..." He would have finished, told his friend all about it, but–

"Oi! We need some beers over here!"

–He was interrupted by a trio of drunkards from down the bar. Earl grunted his displeasure.

"Be back in a minute, Kiddo," he grunted. The old man shambled over to the drunks, favoring his right leg as always. Mike knew that he held no love for these men, for they were little more than burnt out high schoolers that never really grew up. They had little money to pay for their drinks, and even less intelligence to earn them. Mike paused a moment, then picked up his glass off the counter and turned around, searching the bar for an open table near the center of the pub.

As he walked away, Earl looked past his customers and met Mike's eye. Mike raised his glass and nodded an acknowledgment to him. He got halfway to the table before his pants vibrated once, twice, three times. The corners of his mouth tugged into a small smile as he reached into his pocket and withdrew his cell phone. Careful to mind his scotch, he flipped the phone open and read–

--1 New Text Message--

He regarded it for a moment with keen interest, then set it on the nearest table and slid into a chair. Leaving the phone alone for the time being, he yanked a napkin out of the table-top dispenser and set his scotch atop it, an impromptu coaster. Mike closed his eyes and relaxed his shoulder–the stress of the day quickly faded into the background of his mind. He let himself be immersed into the atmosphere of Earl's Pub by God's Gift to College Students—booze—and felt his troubles begin to drown in the stuff.

He sipped his scotch gratefully.

The cell phone perched atop the table he now sat at vibrated once, mocking him—enticing him.

"Just open it." Mike was almost surprised to hear his own voice. "Worst case scenario is she's a psycho with a butcher's knife, right?" Right. He set his glass back on the napkin and snatched up his phone, eager to read.

He opened it and pressed OK to read the thing.

--Thnx 4 a gr8 time last nite. =) Am I going 2 c u 2nite?--

Instantly her smile flashed into his mind—it was not the wide-lipped, toothy grin of modern movie stars, that false projection of happiness and perfection no man should ever hope to come close to, but one of contentment well-earned, a life of hardship transformed to one of happy acceptance of the hardship of life.

Mike took another hit of scotch.

--Menu. Messages. Text Messages--

--Create--

He paused a moment, letting his thumb hover over the keypad, the flashing indicator on a blank screen telling him it was ready to deliver his message. He chose his words carefully, considering the weight, flow, and implications of each word—meticulous, to say the least.

--While I am unable to see you tonight, I tell you so with great disappointment—for I, too, enjoyed our night. I would love to meet with you again, very soon. I am confused though, for your friends called you both Jo and Christina. Who are you?--

He considered the finished message for nearly a minute, wondering if she would take his jest with a laugh or a grimace. He let out a helpless chuckle and pressed SEND. He dropped his phone back onto the table with a clatter that went unheard in the pub, which had just begun to fill with people.

Mike downed the rest of his scotch in a single gulp, a feat he would normally not achieve until he left at midnight, sharp. In the past year, he had made it his habit, his personal norm, to come to Earl's each night and buy a single scotch, which he nursed for four hours before bringing the empty glass back to Earl and bidding him a good night.

Barely a minute and a half after he had sent his message, the phone vibrated again. He smiled and picked it up immediately, this time.

--lol!--

He could hear her laughter in his ears.

--Ya ppl call me all sortsa things. Nicknames ya know? Call me wutever u want 2, handsome--

Mike pondered this a moment. Rather than answering immediately, he stood up from the table and swept the empty glass into his hand. He dropped the phone back into his pocket, then set off, back toward the bar and Earl. When the bartender saw him, he quickly handed two Budweisers to his customer, then waved the man away. Mike took his usual once more and set his glass on the table. Earl stared at him with mock disbelief.

"You're back...for more?"

Mike reached for his wallet to pull out another five, but Earl held his hands up and shook his head.

"This is a momentous occasion! You've finally learned the concept of a refill–this one's on me, Kiddo."

Mike smiled and put his wallet away. Nothing was said as Earl refilled his glass and dropped three fresh ice cubes into it. Mike pulled the renewed glass toward him but didn't bring it to his lips.

"Thanks, Earl." Mike felt Earl's eyes prying at him, but he stared intently at his scotch.

"So–you gonna answer me, or just sit there starin'?" Mike looked up. Earl had his chin propped up by his elbow and he was staring at him. A knowing smile hung on his lips, raising his saggy jowls.

Mike looked at him and raised an eyebrow.

"What's she like?"

She has wide hips and a thin waist, Mike wanted to say, which she flaunted with a subtle flex of her hip with each step. Her posture exuded a genuine self-confidence, an unassuming, easy-going bounce to her step that suggested she'd conquered the worst life could offer–a genuine appreciation for each breath she took, and for the body she was given. She kept her blonde hair cut short, framing her pixie-face perfectly. Her emerald eyes were wide and attentive, and they squinted when she flashed that amazing smile.

"I met her at my buddy's house a few nights back," Mike began. He could tell Earl wanted to make another crack about his lack of social life, but the bartender kept quiet. "I was in the middle of, ah...playin' beer pong when she walked past. I turned to look, Gabe made the serve, and hit me square in the nose–sad thing was, I wasn't even drunk." Mike laughed and shook his head. Earl smiled and nodded. "She laughed a little, hiding behind her hand,

and she had me."

"Love at first laugh, eh? That's a new one, kiddo," Earl said, his words muffled slightly by his hand under his chin.

"No," Mike said firmly, though the bartender wasn't far off. "Not love—but she definitely set that hook pretty well—" he laughed.

Mike's phone vibrated once in his pocket, reminding him he had something to do. He placed his phone on the counter and looked at Earl.

"So? Text her back," the bartender said, and he turned away from Mike to help another customer.

Mike sipped his scotch.

He reviewed the text message one last time, then pressed REPLY.

His fingers flew across the keypad with practiced efficiency, never pausing to think about his actions or his words—he knew exactly what he wanted to say. He backspaced only once, to correct a rogue double punctuation, then pressed SEND without a second thought.

--Perhaps I shall call you mine?--

He smiled and sipped his scotch.

www.ingramcontent.com/pod-product-compliance
Lightning Source LLC
Chambersburg PA
CBHW031607260626
47154CB00020B/1653